RAPUNZEL
AND THE
VANISHING
VILLAGE

BY LEILA HOWLAND

First Hardcover Edition, June 2018
1 3 5 7 9 10 8 6 4 2
FAC-020093-18110
Printed in the United States of America

Designed by Kurt Hartman

Library of Congress Control Number: 2017959432

ISBN 978-1-368-00986-7

Reinforced binding

Visit disneybooks.com

*For Kayla and Vanessa, and the village
we have built together, word by word*
—L.H.

PART ONE

ON THE ROAD

1

RAPUNZEL

"Everyone, I need you to stand still just a little bit longer," I said, using my favorite pencil to add some shading. I wanted to make sure I captured my boyfriend Eugene's features perfectly. "The light is so enchanting and this apple orchard makes a perfect backdrop. I'm almost done. Promise!"

It was the end of our first day on the road. We were on a great journey to save the kingdom of Corona, and I wanted to capture this feeling of a fresh beginning for all time. After all, I'd been longing for escape and for freedom for so long. I'd spent almost eighteen years in a tower and another *much better* year in a castle, inside the walls of Corona. But how many times had I stood on the Corona Wall and gazed at the landscape below, with its rolling hills, flowing rivers, and villages nestled into the verdant countryside, just longing to explore? Too many to count. And now the open road was exactly where we needed to be, for the good of the kingdom.

"Hey, Blondie, you sure this is my best angle?" Eugene asked.

"Yes, Eugene," I said with a laugh. "You're as handsome as ever. Did you get a haircut before we left?"

"More like a style refresh. See, I've been rocking the 'man about the castle' look for almost a year now. It was time for a change now that we're out on the road. I'm going for a rugged look, which is why my goatee is a centimeter longer," Eugene said.

"He looks exactly the same to me," Cass, my best friend and lady-in-waiting said. (She also happened to be the ultimate warrior.)

"I wish I had more opportunities to update my look," Hook Foot said. Hook Foot could usually be found with his friends at the Snuggly Duckling pub and was loyal to Corona. So when he said he wanted to come along, promising to be a helpful assistant, I could hardly say no. "But footwear options are limited. As this adventure into the great unknown begins, I, too, long to express myself. After all, on journeys we have a greater chance of finding ourselves. Perhaps my inner dancer will finally have a chance to twirl."

"Well said, Hook Foot!" I exclaimed. The giddiness of our freedom was clearly affecting all of us.

"Are we almost done here, Princess?" Lance, Eugene's oldest and dearest friend, asked. Eugene and Lance had grown up together as orphans and were like brothers. There was never even a question about whether he would join us on the road. It was a given.

"One more second. The sunset is magical," I said. Just then, Owl, Cass's pet, circled above in the dusk-colored sky. My chameleon, Pascal, waved at him from his perch on my shoulder. The end of the day was approaching.

"Raps, I don't want to ruin the moment," Cass began, "but we need to get back on the road if we're going to stay on schedule. According to my itinerary, we need to get to Deep Canyon before dark and set up camp. That doesn't leave us much time. It's still a ways off."

"But I thought we were stopping to pick these delicious apples," Hook Foot said.

Max whinnied. He was the prize horse of the royal guard. Beside him, Fidella, another one of the kingdom's beloved horses and Max's only true rival in strength and bravery (not to mention his sweetheart!), munched on some grass.

"They deserve a treat for pulling our caravan with such grace and dignity," I said, petting Max's nose.

"My maps don't show another orchard for several miles . . . so that makes sense. But then we should get moving," Cass continued as she opened the back of the caravan and pulled out a barrel. "It's my job to keep us on track and protect us. My wit is just a bonus."

"Depends who you ask," Eugene said. "And I don't think you have the monopoly on protector role, okay, Cassandra?"

"Whatever," Cass said as she started to pick fruit for the horses.

I wondered if I should step in and mention that we were all there to protect one another, that we all contributed wonderful strengths. But sometimes getting involved in Cass and Eugene's disagreements only made things worse. It was hard to know what to do, but since Cass was already distracted by the apples I decided to stay out of it.

"I can also help with security," Hook Foot said, reaching for an apple. "I know you brought me along for my muscles."

"That's right," Eugene said, patting him on the back.

I began to pack up my art supplies, but Eugene rested his hand on mine. "We got this, Blondie. You finish your sketch."

"Thanks, but I want to help," I said.

"Ooh, you nailed my nose!" Eugene said, sneaking a peak at the portrait before I closed my drawing pad. "Not an easy feat! But is this really a group portrait if you're not in it?"

"I'll draw myself in later," I said. "Cass is right. We need to get moving."

Eugene put a hand on my back as we took in the scene before us. The road stretched out like an extended arm. We were at the top of a hill, and I could see Deep Canyon in the distance. A swallow warbled above us. The cool breeze chilled my face. Excitement coursed through my veins. We were really doing this!

But I couldn't ignore the path of sharp black rocks that dotted the road. They reminded me of the mission at hand—that this journey wasn't just about having an adventure; it was about saving Corona. My connection to those spikey formations was mysterious and frightening. They'd made my hair grow back and created chaos in Corona. They were driven by something powerful and

unknown, and they seemed to be leading somewhere. The goal of our quest was to follow them
and get to the bottom of what they were and how
they were connected to me. I was sure that would
bring me to my true destiny. The world was opening up to me for better or worse, or possibly both.

"Raps, we're ready," Cass called. "Are you?"

"Yes," I said, holding my notebook to my chest.
"Yes."

2

CASSANDRA

"'In the far-off land of Aberdinon, I was kept locked up for nearly two months while the snow fell,'" Eugene read, glancing up briefly from the book *The Tales of Flynnigan Rider* he'd borrowed from Corona's library. We were riding side by side on the connected wagons pulled by Max and Fidella. Eugene was deep into the tale, relishing every word. "'People say Aberdinon is flawless, but there's no such thing as flawlessness, and the desire for it belies an emptiness I hope you never know. I can tell you this with great certainty, for I was trapped in this supposed land of perfection, which was really a den of deception, until, through my wits, daring, and'—get this, it may sound familiar—'my *heart-stopping and swoony* smile, I escaped to the port city of Porto.'"

"Swoony?" Raps laughed.

"He's got such a way with words! A creative genius, I say," Eugene said.

"The best there is," said Lance, and he high-fived Eugene.

"Wait a second," I said. "The author of *The Tales of Flynnigan Rider* named a port city *Porto*?"

"Makes total sense to me!" Eugene said.

"It *is* a port," Hook Foot added.

"I just think that the 'creative genius' could have been more . . . creative," I said.

"What's the author's name?" Raps asked.

"The Author," Eugene said, bowing his head reverently. He and Lance did an elaborate handshake that ended with them both howling at the sky. Again, Raps laughed in delight.

"The author's name is *the Author*?" I asked.

"Cass, your owl's name is Owl," Raps said with a smile.

"Touché," I answered with a little grin, despite myself. "But I don't claim to be a creative genius."

"The Author is anonymous," Eugene said. "Adds to his mystique! *Anyway*, back to the story. Ahem! 'Donning a silk robe I'd nicked from the cruel lord's laundry pile, I silently reminded myself of the words that gave me courage time and again as I set out for uncertain lands: *The journey makes me stronger, braver, truer.'* Boy, I love that line!"

"Me too," Raps said.

"Story of our lives, eh, pal?" Lance said, clapping Eugene on the back.

Suddenly, the caravan jolted.

"Something's not right," I said. The connected wagons were tilting and one of the back wheels seemed to be veering.

We careened over a bump in the road and Raps bounced off her seat. "Whoops!" she exclaimed.

"Are you okay?" Eugene asked.

Max and Fidella whinnied as I pulled on the reins and tried to bring us to a halt. They were having a hard time maintaining control, and we were gaining speed.

"Totally fine," Raps said, steadying herself. "In fact, I got this!"

In a swift movement, Raps swung her long inde-structible hair around a branch, slowing us down just as we approached a dip in the road. The horses settled and we came to an easy stop—though the screech of a loose wheel seemed to echo in the hills around us.

Creak.

"Okay, whose job was it to check the wheels before we left?" I asked.

"Let's focus on the here and now. I bet if we work together we can fix this," Raps said.

"Unless it's unfixable," Lance mused. "That would be unfortunate."

"Um, can we at least try to stay positive?" Raps asked.

"Don't panic," I said, though my own heart was beating fast. It would not be good if the caravan needed more than a quick fix. But I would figure it out.

"I . . . wasn't," Raps said.

"I wasn't, either," Hook Foot chimed in.

"Was anyone here in a panic?" Lance asked, glancing around.

"I'm not going to say that was enjoyable—" Eugene started, but I cut him off.

"We can still get to our first stop on time. According to my maps, we have room for an error here and there. It's not like I don't know how to plan an itinerary," I said, hopping off the caravan. "I'd better check out the problem."

"I'll help," Eugene said.

"That won't be necessary," I replied. It was fun to hear his stories, but I didn't have time to deal with his ego when it came to the business of keeping us on track. I searched my belongings. There had to be something in my stash that would work to strengthen the attachment of the wheel to the caravan.

"You know, I'm pretty handy, actually," Eugene said, leaning against the side of the wagon.

"Aha!" I said, retrieving a hammer. I could probably secure the attachments with a good pounding—at least enough to get us to Deep Canyon without risking losing all our earthly possessions before nightfall.

"Are you sure you don't want my advice?" Eugene asked.

"Listening to friends never hurts. . . ." Raps added.

"Hi-yah!" I took a swing at the attachment, ignoring them.

"Whoa," Eugene said, fear crossing his face. "Nothing good is accomplished under stress, Cassandra. Maybe you should take a deep breath, step aside, and—"

"Eugene, it's dangerous to be on the road after dark with the princess of Corona," I said.

"Hey, hey now," he said. "Who's the guy here who actually lived on the road for most of his life?"

"Uh . . . me?" Lance asked.

"Okay, *guys*," Eugene said. "I know that these parts are clear of thieves."

"And how do you determine that?" I asked as I adjusted the clasp.

"Because we're so exposed," Eugene said. "Look around. Are there any big hedges or leafy trees for these undesirable characters to hide in?"

I wiped the sweat from my brow as I continued to pound away, hoping to create a stronger link between the peg and the hole.

"No robber worth his salt would take the high road," Lance agreed.

"Raps," I said. "Do you want to get to a secure campsite in Deep Canyon or are you just fine and dandy out here in the open, without so much as a bush to conceal us should some thieves come sneaking by?"

"I've never been on the road before," she said, "so maybe Eugene and Lance are right. Nothing looks dangerous. . . ."

"Well, she's a perpetual optimist," I said. "But the princess will not be out after dark, at least not on my watch."

I was Raps's protector. She was a strong girl, no doubt, but the king had entrusted me with her safety. If I couldn't protect her, then who would I be?

"Cassandra, are you even considering what I said?" Eugene remarked.

The wind shifted. I glanced up. Owl was circling in a northeasterly direction, drawing my attention to the darkening clouds.

"It's also going to rain," I said. "And who knows for how long. Maybe as long as a week."

"Possibly," Eugene said, glancing up. "But it's not like we'll feel it in our caravans. Oh, and by the way, you're never going to be able to fix that wheel without some leverage," Eugene said.

"Stick to your coiffure," I muttered.

"Okay, well, we'll be here all night. Without leverage you might as well be swimming upstream with a paddle between your teeth."

"That's just weird," I said.

"I think working as a team is the way to go," Raps said.

"I'm just talking about a few inches," Eugene continued.

Without even thinking, I grabbed the Flynn Rider book from under his arm, stuck it under the clasp, and gave it a good whack. To my surprise, the peg slipped right back into place.

"I fixed it!" I said.

"Except, what about the part where I . . ." Eugene started. "And hey, that's my favorite book."

But I was too focused on getting us back on course to respond to him. I squinted at the remains of the sun, which was slinking into the valley like an egg yolk. With the caravan hitched properly, we'd be in Deep Canyon in no time. We were still on track. No loose wheels or bad weather could stop us now. I jumped back in the driver's seat, gestured for everyone to hop aboard, and called out to Fidella and Max.

"Onward!"

3

EUGENE

"Ahhh! Here we are: Deep Canyon!" I said, standing tall and gesturing to the great expanse of land under the night sky around us. "And all is well—not a ruffian, thief, or thug in sight." I gave my own swoony smile and raised an eyebrow at Rapunzel, who glanced up and waved in return. We'd gathered around a cozy fire and she was hard at work on her portrait again.

"Really? I've got a pretty clear view of a few right now," Cass said, glancing back and forth between Lance, Hook Foot, and me.

"Very funny, Cass," I said. "*Verrrry* funny. You know, in one of my favorite stories by the Author,

Flynn Rider says that humor is the tightest bond among travelers."

"I love that!" Rapunzel said.

"And, by the by, I'm not a thief. My record has been expunged." I winked at my girl and used a stick to prod the fire. The flames jumped to life, giving Rapunzel the light I knew she needed for her sketch.

"Thanks," she said, glancing up at me. I smiled. She looked lovely in the firelight.

"And I don't know a ruffian who can prepare a meal like this," Lance said, opening the lid of the pot to reveal his famous vegetable stew. "Ratatouille with grains, garnished with freshly picked herbs and a dash of je ne sais quoi!"

"That was me," Hook Foot said. "I gathered the herbs. This hook comes in handy in ways you wouldn't imagine."

"I think I just lost my appetite," Cass said.

"Princesses first," I said.

"That's okay," Rapunzel said, focusing on her drawing. "Serve me last. I'm still trying to get a few details right."

Cass put her hand over Raps's bowl. "Are you sure these herbs aren't poisonous?"

"Looks like herbs to me," Hook Foot said with a shrug.

"That's not good enough. If Rapunzel gets sick on our first night on the road because of some misidentified weeds, you can be sure—" Cassandra started.

"Will you calm down, Calamity Cass?" I said. I sprinkled some of Hook Foot's herbs in my hand, examined them for texture, and gave them a good sniff. "Wild chives." I popped a handful into my mouth.

Pascal nodded to a lightly roasted fly in front of him. I sprinkled some herbs on his dish, and he licked his lips with delight. "The frog likes it."

"How do I know you won't be plagued by stomach ailments in, say, twenty minutes?" Cass asked.

Rapunzel crossed something out, her brow furrowed.

"Cassandra," I tried again, "the road is where I grew up. And I don't think you can find anyone here complaining about my good looks, strength, or intelligence, am I right, Rapunzel?"

"Definitely," Rapunzel sighed, frowning at the picture. She was immersed in her art. "I can't get my portrait to look right. Something's off."

I sprinkled chives over my dish in a show of confidence and then looked at her drawing.

"See, I'm trying to add myself to the picture," Rapunzel said.

"It looks like you," I said. "Kind of."

"It feels so stiff," Rapunzel said.

"It's been a long day," I said, trying to put her at ease.

"And this light isn't great," Cass said. "Maybe you can try again tomorrow?"

Cass and I nodded at each other. Encouraging Rapunzel was something we could agree on.

"I guess so," Rapunzel said. She put the pencil down and tasted her stew. "Mmm . . . this is delicious!"

Just then, I felt a cold drop on my head and then another on my shoulder.

"Told you rain was coming," Cass said, leaping up. "Rapunzel, take shelter. Hook Foot, cover the firewood and collect the food. Lance, make sure the caravan windows are shut and watertight."

Boy, Cassandra really liked ordering us around.

"I'll set up the shelter for the horses," I called as I stood up, helping Rapunzel gather her art supplies. I opened the girls' wagon door for her to climb inside.

"No, I'm already doing that," Cassandra said. "You just . . . stay out of the way."

"Stay out of the way?" I asked.

"Fine. You want a job? Clean the dishes," Cassandra said in a huff.

Dish duty? If only she could have seen me in the old days, I thought.

"I'm perfectly capable of helping, too," Rapunzel said.

"Of course you are," I said. "But it looks like we've got this covered. And I'm sure Cass will have us back on the trail of the black rocks first thing in the morning. You should get some rest." We all knew that as much as we were there to help and support our girl, it would ultimately be Rapunzel who would solve the mystery of the rocks and save the kingdom.

"Good point," Rapunzel said with a soft smile.

I went to rinse the plates in a nearby creek, the rain soaking my clothes, while the others tended to drier tasks. I wondered what the point was of washing anything in the rain. Then I wondered what had gone wrong that no one seemed to appreciate my skills. Earlier that day, I'd lent my expertise on how to find the best shortcuts through the forest, and Cass had told me to sweep the caravans' stoops instead. And then to sort our stores of tea leaves. This was life on the open road! I had a lot more to offer here. Had castle life softened my edges?

What a day, I thought, packing up the last of the now-sparkling dishes just as a fleet of squirrels hurried past, spraying mud on my pants . . . and the plates.

Later, tucked in my bed inside the boys' wagon, I tried to nod off, deciding the next day would be a chance to start over. But it didn't help that Lance snored like a bear—with a megaphone.

"How'd you sleep?" I asked Rapunzel the next morning. We were the first two out of the wagons. She was sketching again, but from the look of things, she was still struggling. I sat down beside her.

"Not so great," she said, leaning into me. Her lower lip turned down. "Even with turning in early."

"Oh, no," I said, and hugged her. "What happened?"

"There was a leak," she replied. "Right over my head. I feel like I was in a battle with it all night. No matter how many times I plugged it, it won. Drip. Drip. Drip—right into my ear. Pascal's thumb was the only thing that stopped the water. But the poor guy needed to go to bed, too."

Pascal was now curled on her lap, fast asleep.

"Maybe I could have handled things differently," she said. "I should have made sure everyone would be dry and well-rested when we prepared the caravan."

"You did great. We all thought the wagons were secure," I said.

"But I should have checked for leaks," she sighed. "And for unsteady wheels."

"Did you get any shut-eye at all?" I asked.

"A few hours, maybe. We finally just put a bowl under it and slept on the floor," she said.

Luckily, it had stopped raining, though the sky was still cloudy and threatening.

"I'm sorry. But the wheel is fine now, and I'll fix that roof today," I said, planning to take a look before Cass could do it herself and put me on trash duty or something. "Kind of makes you miss Corona, doesn't it?"

She nodded. "A little too much," she said, biting her lip. "Eugene, you don't think all of this—the wheel, the rain, my sketch—are signs that we're not on the right path here, do you? I thought I wanted adventure, but nothing seems to be going the way it's supposed to. How will this journey end if the beginning is already kind of falling apart?"

"Oh, all that?" I said, holding her close. "That's just part of the fun! The color, the *character* that'll make the tales of our adventures that much better."

Rapunzel brightened. "You know, you're right, Eugene. And I'm so relieved you know how to fix leaks," she said. "That's a start."

"Of course. I know all about life on the road, though sometimes I get the feeling that Cassandra doesn't believe I can handle anything but boring chores."

"I'm really hoping you two can get along," she said. "I know it's hard, but you have more in common than you think. Maybe we're *all* just feeling a bit homesick."

"Absolutely," I said.

"Thank you." Rapunzel placed a hand on my cheek and said, "And I know you did the most important job of all last night."

"What's that?" I asked.

"You saved my art supplies from the rain, and that means the world to me," she said, and then she hugged me.

"Good morning, lovebirds!" Lance said, announcing himself with the volume of a well-rested man.

"Morning!" Rapunzel said. We both seemed to be feeling better after having shared a few moments alone. I squeezed her a little more tightly.

Lance handed Rapunzel and me two steaming cups of tea as Hook Foot emerged from the caravan.

"Rough night last night, huh?" Lance said.

"What are you talking about, man?" I asked. "You snored like a beast from the minute your head hit the pillow until just now."

"I didn't hear a thing," Hook Foot said. "I put socks in my ears."

"Neat trick," I said.

"I only got a measly seven and a half hours of sleep," Lance explained. "I need a full eight or I get testy."

"It wasn't a great night for me, either," Cassandra said as she climbed out of the caravan.

"Were you awake, too?" Rapunzel asked.

"No, but I had some bad dreams about losing my weapons," Cassandra said. "It's my worst nightmare to be unprepared."

"You know what we need?" Lance said, slapping his knee.

"To turn around?" Hook Foot asked.

"Nope! Good old-fashioned comfort. Let's stop and see Grandma Pearl," Lance said. "Also known as Pearly Perlson."

"I don't know what's more surprising," I said, stroking my goatee. "That you have a grandma or that her name is Pearly Perlson."

"No blood relation," Lance replied with a straight face. "That's just the name an old thieving pal goes by. After we went our separate ways, Eugene, I had to make other friends. Pearly was one of the best of them. She fed me for a month when I was in a bad way. We took so kindly to each other that she told me I could call her grandma. Rumor has it that she's gone on the straight and narrow like us. She's got a roadside stand called Pearl's Provisions. Her cooking will definitely get our road trip back on track."

"Rolls off the tongue," I said. "Pearl's Provisions."

"I guess I could use some extra time to perfect my maps," Cassandra said.

Rapunzel smiled at me and I pressed her hand.

No more boring chores? Some good eats? A less cranky Cass?

Things were looking up.

4

RAPUNZEL

"**G**et yer fried fiddleheads, boiled peanuts, and mustard-crusted mollusks, right here at Pearl's Provisions!" called the tiny, withered woman from a stool perched next to a roadside stand bearing her name. "Wash 'em down with some fresh sassafras root beer, brewed to perfection!"

I laughed a little as the wagons slowed in front of the ramshackle structure. Grandma Pearl probably weighed about ninety-seven pounds and had a head of wild hair. She had large brown eyes, a wide smile, and a swagger that rivaled Eugene's. In her pantaloons and poet's blouse, she was quite a sight!

"Grandma Pearl!" I shouted as I leapt from the

wagon. I gave her a big bear hug and a kiss on her soft cheek.

"You plant those walking sticks right where they are, missy-with-a-mane," she said, backing away and wagging a finger at me. "As far as I know I don't have a grandchild. There's only one person who I let call me grandma, and he's a man of quite different stature. I may be short of vision and hard of hearing, but if you think I'm going to fall for some half-baked granny routine and give you free cricket cookies or dandelion ice cream, you picked the wrong biddy to bicker with!"

"Relax, Grandma Pearl!" Lance said, approaching with outstretched arms. "It's me, Lance. These are my friends!"

Grandma Pearl narrowed her eyes and took a cautious step closer.

"Well, I'll be!" Grandma Pearl exclaimed as Cass hitched up the horses and the rest of our group gathered around. "If it isn't my sweet li'l peanut pie, Fancy Lancy, finally come to pay his friend a visit." They embraced and Lance lifted her high off the ground and spun her around. She squealed with delight. "Why didn't you say you were coming before I gave this fuzzy peach"—she pointed a thumb at me—"a vocal knock 'em, sock 'em, down-in-the-dirt, one-two punch, Pearly-style."

28

"We just started a road trip, and I thought we should pay you a visit before we got to our next stop," Lance explained.

"I guess I understand," Grandma Pearl said, waving Lance off. "But you know me! I'd have liked to prepare a meal for you and your travel companions." She leaned in closer to Lance and whispered, "They are companions, aren't they? You aren't back into the low-life thieving anymore, are ya?"

Lance shook his head no.

"Good!" she cried, throwing an arm around him. "Me neither. I'm flying low and keeping cool. Would ya get a look at us? From a troublemaking twosome to a do-right duo! Who'da guessed?"

Lance beamed.

"We didn't mean to alarm you, Mrs. Perlson," I said.

"It's miss, honeybun. I'm not married."

"Oh, pardon me, Miss Perlson!" I said.

"Call me Pearly. And it's okay, lassie long locks," she replied. "You're stayin' for dinner, aren't ya?"

"Grandma, this is the princess Rapunzel," Lance said.

"Princess?" Granny asked.

I nodded and smiled.

"Well, hi-dee-ho!" she exclaimed and slapped her knee. "Fancy Lancy indeed! You've certainly moved up in society! I'll tell you what, the creek down there is running high and the fish are jumping. If y'all go get us some fish, I'll close up shop and start the fire. We'll have a feast in no time. It'll be royally fun. Get it?"

"I do!" I said, laughing. Pearly's enthusiasm was contagious. "I've never been fishing before."

"I can catch a fish," Cass said, approaching us.

"All righty, whippersnapper!" Pearly said, slapping her on the back and handing her a pole. "Have at 'em."

"And as one who's lived on the road, I'm no stranger to fishing for my supper," Eugene said, smiling broadly and extending his hand. "Eugene Fitzherbert. I'm honored to meet you, Pearly."

"Well, hello there, handsome," Pearly said, fluffing her hair. "Lance told me about you—but he failed to mention how pretty you are! You single?"

"Grandma Pearl!" Lance said, wincing with embarrassment.

"Actually, he's taken," I said, and linked my arm through Eugene's.

"Figures," Pearly said. She sniffed and cocked an eyebrow. "All the good ones are."

"It's true I'm with her," Eugene said. "Though you are clearly a woman of true beauty and excellent taste."

"Lucky for me, it's still free to look!" Pearly said with a laugh. "Now, get yourselves down to that creek before the sun sets, and I'll meet you by the fire pit. I'd offer you a room in my house tonight, but all I have is a pallet on the floor above the shop."

"We'll be just fine in our caravan," I told her as we headed for the river.

"Take this here bucket!" she called after us. "And don't come back till it's full!"

5

CASSANDRA

We heard the creek before we saw it. It was deep in the forest, lined by trees with low, stretching branches and ferns with green fronds. It was wide and shady, and the water parted around the stepping-stones where frogs perched and sun gleamed. The best thing about the sight was the roaring waterfall, which created a layer of white foam in the creek below.

"Wow," Raps said. "Just . . . wow! Okay, this makes up for last night!"

"Amazing!" Eugene added, taking her hand.

"The whole area is known for waterfalls," I said. "I'm definitely going to mark this one on my map."

"I'm thinking it's swim time," Raps said. "In fact,

as the princess, I formally declare it to be swim-ming hour!"

"Can't ignore a royal command," I said, and sat down to take off my boots. Raps had made a good call. The swiftly moving water was too difficult to resist after another long day on the road. Raps and I loved swimming together, ever since we'd discov-ered the Lost Lagoon back in Corona. It was where we'd become best friends. She'd taught me how to swim, and I'd told her all about the history of the kingdom. Later, we'd been able to piece together a mystery that had eluded Coronans for centuries. Swimming was sort of our thing.

"Let's all slide down that waterfall together," Raps said, stepping into the rushing water. "Oooh, it's cold, really, really, really cold, but wonderful!"

It was.

Eugene, Lance, and Hook Foot followed as we made our way along the ledge of the waterfall.

"Take hands," Raps instructed. Reluctantly, I took Eugene and Hook Foot's hands.

"One, two, three . . ." Raps counted, and then we were off, flying through the air and landing in the deep, frothing water below.

After an hour of fun, we took turns with the fish-ing pole, trying to catch our dinner.

"Looks like that storm hasn't quite passed," I said as dark clouds crossed the sky.

"Don't ruin the mood, Cass," Eugene said.

Then Lance piped up. "I sure am in the mood for a good old-fashioned story while we wait for the fish to bite."

"That's a great idea, Lance," Eugene said. "Something with adventure?"

"And daring?" Lance asked.

"And a whole lot of fun?" I said.

"You know it," Lance said.

"I can see where this is headed," I said.

"Flynn Rider!" Lance and Eugene shouted together.

"We left off at an exciting part—Flynn had escaped to Porto," Rapunzel said. "Tell us the rest of it!"

"Let's see if I still remember it by heart," Eugene said. "'A frosty wind blew off the ocean, and I prepared myself to face the pirates who were docked in Porto. As rough as they were with their rotted teeth and salty breath, their ships would be most hospitable to a rogue like myself, looking for a ride to my dear, sweet home in the peaceful village of Harmony Glen. I found a sharp rock to serve as an emergency weapon—'"

"Wait, did you say Harmony Glen?" I asked.

"Yes," I said. "Now if you don't mind, Cass, there's a little something called momentum . . ."

"No, it's just that name rings a bell," I said. I dug through my satchel.

"Of course it rings a bell!" Eugene said. "Anyone who's read the Flynn Rider stories knows Harmony Glens is the town where the Author lived and created his immortal character."

"In all the stories, Flynn goes out on wild adventures, but always returns to Harmony Glen," Lance said. "The Author described it as a melting pot of ideas and cultures."

"Where traders from many kingdoms met to exchange goods and services," Eugene added. "Thieving was everywhere, but so were music, dance, and feasts that went on for days."

"I bet the travelers were able to teach each other the crafts of their lands," Rapunzel said. "The art must have been incredible."

"So, it's a real place? The Author didn't bother to change the name of the town?" I asked.

"It's called *Harmony Glen!*" Eugene said. "You can't change a name like that."

"Hmmm . . ." I unfolded the oldest map of the area I'd been able to find before I left the kingdom. Then I took out a sturdier piece of parchment—an official map given to us by the king the day we set out. "That's so odd. It's clearly marked on my *old* map, the one I found in the library," I said, pointing to the middle of the dusty piece of paper. "But it's not on this one." I unrolled the newer map.

"I have to see this," Eugene said. "Holy moly! Harmony Glen! I can't believe it."

"It doesn't look that far from where we are," Raps said. "Am I right, Cass?"

"Maybe only five miles or so," I said.

"Wait . . . what?" Eugene exclaimed. "Harmony Glen is only five miles from here? We need to go! I have to see where Flynn Rider was created."

"Me too," Lance said. "In a way, Harmony Glen is the closest thing Eugene and I had to a home growing up, even if it was only in our minds."

"I think there's something in my eye," Eugene said, wiping away a tear.

"But look," I said, holding up the official map. "There's no sign of it on here."

"It . . . vanished?" Hook Foot asked.

"That's impossible," Raps said. "An entire village just . . . disappeared?"

"Sounds like we need to investigate," Eugene said.

"No, no, no," I said, realizing what I'd started. "There's no way we're taking another detour."

"It would mean so much to me," Eugene said.

"I based my former identity on this guy, after all. Harmony Glen is supposed to be one of the most beautiful and inspirational places on earth! It's like its very own world, with its own species of flowers and this really cool bog!"

"Cool bog? Is that a thing?" I asked.

"I've never seen a bog," Rapunzel said.

"Then you haven't lived!" Eugene said.

"What's a bog?" Hook Foot asked.

"A bog! It's kind of like a marsh. Lots of stuff grows there," Eugene said.

"Weird stuff," I added. "With flora like sledges and heaths."

"English, please?" Lance remarked, leaning on his elbow.

"Plants in all stages of life," I amended. "The materials are rich with nutrients and can be put to many uses."

"I'd love to see that," Raps said.

"Sounds pretty," Hook Foot agreed.

"No way," I said. "Sorry."

"Let's talk about this as a team," Rapunzel said.

I glanced at her. Of course, she ultimately was the leader of this expedition. But I had worked so hard to make the most efficient itinerary.

"Oh, c'mon, Cassandra. Harmony Glen is said to be a slice of heaven," Eugene said.

"Visiting Pearly for a meal is one thing, but going out of our way for swamp sightseeing is another," I said. "We need to follow the rocks."

Raps nodded thoughtfully. "I think she's right, Eugene. Sorry," she said. "Even though Harmony Glen sounds intriguing."

"The legend says that the air in Harmony Glen is actually different because of the unique terrain," Eugene said. "I mean, just throwing it out there. . . ."

"It's been known to inspire some of the greatest stories ever written," Lance added with a raised eyebrow.

Just then, a fish bit.

"Maybe that's a sign!" Raps said.

I pulled on the straining fishing pole and discovered I'd caught a fish large enough to feed a family of six.

"It's huge!" Raps said. "Way to go, Cass!"

"I've got one, too!" Eugene said, holding up a net he had fashioned with sticks and some weeds.

"And me!" Hook Foot lifted that hook of his to reveal his own catch.

If it was a sign, it was a big one. The fish kept coming. We each caught several: me with the pole, Raps using her hair, Eugene with his net, Hook Foot with his hook, and Lance with his bare hands.

We collected our dinner in the bucket and headed back to Pearly's, each of us newly energized and wondering what lay in store.

Later, as we were seated in a circle around the fire pit with Grandma Pearl, the flames from the cooking fire lit up our faces and the smell of fish frying in oil, onion, and garlic filled the air. We devoured the fresh fish, topping our plates with fiddlehead ferns, which basically tasted like asparagus. Only Lance tried Pearly's cricket cookies. I might have been able to handle fifty different weapons, but eating insects? No thanks.

"What do you know about Harmony Glen?" Raps asked.

"Mmm, Harmony Glen," Pearly said as she sipped her tin mug of sassafras root beer. "Heck of a place."

"It's not on the newer maps," I said, "which is very odd. . . ."

"Unless it's a place that don't want to be found," Pearly said with wide eyes.

"I've always been a big fan of the Flynn Rider stories," Eugene said.

"Adventure, suspense, and colorful language," Pearly replied. "How could you not love those tales? I know I always have."

"Have you ever been there?" Lance asked.

"Absolutely, though not for many long years," Pearly said.

"Tell us about it," Eugene said.

"Yes, we want to know what it's like," Raps said.

"And exactly how far from here is it?" I asked, knowing where this was headed. "In miles."

"It's only a few miles away, if you can find the north entrance that is, and unfortunately, all I can do is tell you how it used to be."

"We'd love to hear . . ." Raps said.

"It was a lively place, always a-buzzing and a-jumping, like lard on a hot griddle. Why, traders and travelers, performers and musicians, from north, south, east, and west, all crossed paths in Harmony Glen. How else do you think the Author learned of so many foreign lands and customs?" Pearly asked, raising an eyebrow as she peered over her mug.

"By traveling the world," Eugene said. "That's what I've always imagined."

"Sorry, handsome, but they say he rarely left home," Pearly explained as she used a long stick to stoke the fire. "Instead, he listened to the stories of the people passing through—and many people did. There were healing waters there."

"The bog!" Eugene shouted.

"You got it, good lookin'," Pearly said. "That bog

contains moss that's known to do everything from healing wounds to transforming into a metal stronger than iron. And it's pretty as a picture to boot."

"I thought bogs were kind of like swamps," I said.

"This is the nicest swamp you ever did see," Pearly said. "And it keeps the air clean and temperature mild."

"Sounds like a kind of paradise," Rapunzel said.

"Well, it wasn't all folk dancin' and fricassee frog legs," Pearly said. "Thieving was rampant, they had a prowler problem, and no one was in charge. It was a lawless place." Pearly yawned. "Ooh-eee! It's about time for me to hit the straw."

"Grandma Pearl, you can't go to bed before you tell us what happened to Harmony Glen," Lance said.

"The great storm hit . . . oh, about fifteen years ago," Pearly said as she rubbed her eyes. "Without anyone in charge down there, the flooding just wiped the town out. Carried the taverns straight out to sea. At least, that's what they say. They built up some walls and now no one comes or goes from that area very often. If I were still thieving, I'd say the territory is ripe for a revisit. But that's not my game any longer. I stick to provisions."

"So, what's in its place now?" I asked, intrigued

in spite of myself. "An entire town can't just disappear from the world, no matter what's on the maps."

"I haven't reason to go lookin' and nobody much talks about it anymore," Pearly said. "Last I heard, someone finally did step up and take charge. He's the one who built the walls. Doesn't sound like much fun to me. I just try to stay in business, feeding the traffic from Corona to Vardaros. Now, it's time for me to put my pigs up and catch some sleep."

"Thank you," Rapunzel said. "We're so grateful for your hospitality."

"Anytime, peachy princess," Pearly said.

"Yes, thank you for the delicious meal," I said. Then I excused myself.

As the rest of them bantered for a little bit longer, I pulled out my maps in the girls' wagon, studying the differences between the old one with Harmony Glen and the new one with a glaring empty space, marked only by cross-hatching—the sort a cartographer would use to indicate an expanse of land gone fallow.

If we had all the time in the world, if the mystery of the rocks weren't so important, I would have spent all the time it took to fill in that map until it was an accurate portrayal of the land. But we had a schedule, a plan. I had a princess to protect. And yet . . . curiosity was brimming inside me like a lake filled with fresh rainwater.

What happened to you, Harmony Glen? I wondered.

I traced my finger over a possible route to the northernmost point, which I imagined would be where the entrance was. I supposed it wouldn't be so terrible to make another pit stop. Just to check things out and make sure everything was all right. It might be good information for the king and queen to have when we returned. Nothing was better than an up-to-date map.

I took out my itinerary and scribbled in a few amendments.

Rapunzel would be excited, at least.

6

RAPUNZEL

"Whoa, Fidella," I said, pulling on the horse's reins to slow her down.

Something odd was happening. In front of us appeared to be a naturally occurring cascade of vines. But the breeze that had been caressing my face and winding through my long hair for most of the morning's journey stopped blowing too quickly. It seemed we had arrived.

"This is the spot on the old map," Cass said as we came to a complete stop.

"And this is the giant wall Grandma Pearl told us about," Eugene said. With the agility of a cat, he climbed the vines until he was thirty feet above the ground.

"Let's find the way in," Cass said, determined.

Eugene turned around and exclaimed, "Flying Flynnigans! This is it!"

"What do you mean?" I asked, swinging my hair around a high branch. Cass grinned and nodded, then grabbed my hand as we jumped together.

"It's gorgeous, it's stunning. It's beyond what I expected," he went on, still staring out in front of him. "Blondie, I really have to share this—"

"View?" I said as Cass and I landed right next to him on top of the huge wall. I was high up, but my feet were strong beneath me, grounding me and allowing me to stand tall. Once again, I felt ready for adventure.

His face lit up and we stepped closer together. "You know, that trick never gets old." I leaned into him as we gazed at the land before us. There were rolling hills, winding streams, patches of bright wildflowers, and small cottages dotting the impossibly green grass. In the distance was a forest, and I imagined the bog to be nestled somewhere in there.

"It certainly is beautiful," I said.

"But not exactly the loud and joyful meeting of cultures Eugene described. It seems kind of empty," Cass pointed out.

"This is just the entrance," Eugene said. "We have to see what's inside."

"I'm so glad we found it. We would have missed this place if we hadn't been looking for it," I said.

"Hey, you three up there," Lance shouted from below. "We found the gate."

The entrance to Harmony Glen was so charming that I had to stop the caravan after we made our way through the unlocked gate, which was covered in vines, to make a quick sketch. Two magnificent oaks marked the smooth road that, according to Cass's old map, would lead us right into the heart of Flynn Rider's legendary home. Hanging between the trees was a sign that read *Harmony Glen* in beautiful script, painted in gold. The artist had decorated it so it appeared to be woven with vines and roses.

I pulled out my colored pencils and tried to capture the scene: the majestic trees, the bright green grass, the hills behind them—which were oddly symmetrical, as though the artist hadn't stopped at the sign but instead had continued to create the land around it, leaving no detail out—not even the cute little bunnies that were bounding through the grass.

"What'd I tell you?" Eugene asked.

"It's so pretty!" I said.

"Anyone can have a nice entrance," Cassandra

said. "What's pretty on the outside isn't necessarily pretty on the inside."

"This is beautiful, Eugene," I said. The night before, when I'd put my art supplies away and Pascal and I had gotten ready for bed, it had occurred to me that I was thinking too much, and that was why I couldn't quite get myself right when I was drawing. Maybe I needed to work as quickly as possible and my artistic instincts would kick in. I sketched quickly as the light shifted from the clouds parting above, creating a lovely dappled effect on the ground around us.

"I thought you said it was going to rain again, Cass," Hook Foot said.

"Yeah, looks like the weather really cleared up," Lance added. We all looked behind us, where the clouds had gathered. Yet there in Harmony Glen it was a picture-perfect day.

"Must be something about this place that brings out the sunshine—hopefully in people, too," Eugene said. "I don't know what Pearly was talking about, Lance. This place *is* thriving."

As the caravan rolled down the road leading to the village, the scene seemed to get even more beautiful—and more populated. Pleasant-looking townspeople waved to us, all wearing the same cornflower blue dresses or pants.

"Hi!" I said, waving cheerfully.

Everyone seemed happy and busy. Children planted gardens. A man gathered vegetables. Two women rode horses. Another group of children looked like they were practicing steps for some kind of country line dance.

"I have to say, Harmony Glen is . . ." I started, unable to find the word I was searching for.

"Unbelievable," Cass said, though it was hard to tell if she meant that in a good or bad way.

"Are you Princess Rapunzel?" a sweet-looking girl with dimples asked as she ran alongside the caravan. She had been collecting flowers in a basket. She wore a cute white bonnet.

"Yes," I said. "How did you know?"

"Your hair, of course," she answered.

I laughed, touching my mane. "Sometimes I forget about it." Pascal gave a formal bow from my shoulder.

"And who are you?" I asked.

"I'm Daphne," she said. "Welcome!" She threw out her arms, shaking her basket. "Can I braid your hair later?"

"Of course! And be careful of your flowers, Daphne! Looks like you're dropping some!" I said.

"Here," she said, and handed me a plump pink tulip.

"Oh, thank you, it's gorgeous!" I said.

"Is that your prince?" she asked, her eyes growing wide at Eugene's smile.

"Um . . . Not yet. I mean, yes, kind of? I mean . . ."
Pascal looked from me to Eugene and back to me.

Oh gosh! I bit my lip and felt my cheeks grow warm. Though Eugene had proposed a year earlier, I just wasn't ready to be married yet. I had so much to see and do—like this road trip. So we were taking our time, and Eugene, being the wonderful boyfriend that he was, understood. But that didn't mean things weren't a little bit awkward from time to time.

"He's a very handsome servant, Princess," Daphne whispered.

"He's not my servant," I said. She looked confused. "He's my very special friend." Eugene grimaced. Cass stifled a laugh. "Special friend. Most special friend of all time." I cleared my throat, deciding to change the subject. "Um, can you tell us where we can find the leader here?" I asked. "We'd like to introduce ourselves."

"Sure," Daphne said. "If you follow this road, you'll come across the village council's meeting spot, the leadership pavilion."

We followed the path Daphne had pointed out. I mentally rehearsed what I was going to say: *Hello,*

I am Princess Rapunzel of Corona. Apologies for not sending word ahead of our visit, but we are excited to see your charming village. This was one of the first times I would represent the kingdom on my own; I wanted to do it the right away.

But when we got to the pavilion, I realized I might not need my speech after all. It looked like someone had told them about our arrival. A quartet of fiddlers greeted us, leading a group of dancers. A small crowd of waving villagers stood nearby.

I beamed at Eugene. This was delightful. Cass remained stoic. Hook Foot tapped his hook in time to the beat and Lance swung Daphne on his shoulders. The fiddlers parted and some people dressed in crisp suits emerged from the pavilion.

One of them, a very tall man with the whitest teeth I'd ever seen, stepped forward.

"Princess Rapunzel," he said, and bowed deeply. "I am Joaquin, and this is the village council. We welcome you to Harmony Glen from the bottoms of our hearts."

"That's so kind," I said. "This has been a warm greeting to be certain. A little girl named Daphne gave me this tulip, and then there was the music and the dancers—it's almost as if you knew we were coming."

"We are so honored you chose to visit us."

"This isn't really a social call," Cass said under her breath. I nudged her. "What?" she muttered, and then stood up straight and looked him squarely in the eye. "Harmony Glen was very hard to find."

"I know," Joaquin said. "We've been meaning to trim back those hedges and add a great sign with our new town emblem, but other business has gotten in the way. You'll be happy to know that we've almost finished the emblem and are planning on revealing it soon."

Cass narrowed her eyes. Joaquin squirmed. He seemed unaccustomed to not being able to win people over.

"This visit was all Eugene's idea," I said, changing the subject.

Eugene stepped forward and held out his hand for a shake.

"The legendary Eugene Fitzherbert," Joaquin said, brightening. They shook hands.

"You've heard of me?" Eugene asked.

"Yes! Of course, we all knew that the moniker Flynn Rider was being used by a talented thief—" Joaquin began.

"Redistributor of nonessential items," Lance interjected.

"Well, if you think word didn't spread through the land that this very man, later revealed to be named Eugene Fitzherbert, was the current beau of the Princess Rapunzel," Joaquin continued, "you're a walnut!"

I had to laugh. A walnut!

"And it's true what they say about you!" Joaquin went on. "Abigail? Martina? Alfonso? Don't you agree?" He turned to his companions.

"Most certainly," Abigail said.

"Without a doubt," Martina added. "Right, Alfonso?"

"The spitting image," Alfonso said.

"I'm not sure what you mean," Eugene said.

"Why, you're an exact replica!" Joaquin said.

"Whose replica?" Eugene said.

"Get over it," Cass said. "They're obviously talking about Flynn Rider."

Cass gestured to the statue in front of the pavilion. Even though Flynnigan Rider was a fictional character, the Author had also illustrated the books, and there was a clear resemblance between his renderings and Eugene. But it had never been more obvious than in this statue, which the Author himself had created.

"I guess there is a . . . resemblance," Eugene said, starting to grin.

"It's more than a resemblance, it's a perfect match. Eugene, I feel as though Flynn Rider has finally come home. I hope you'll all be able to stay for Flynnigan Rider Festival? It's just a few short days away, and your presence will most certainly bring happiness to our little glen."

Eugene's smile shone as bright as the Harmony Glen sunlight. This was just what we needed— some joy and inspiration. What better way to get it than to spend a few days in an adorable village whose hero touted the importance of adventure? It could help us reenergize and get into a good mindset for our ultimate mission.

If I was being honest, I really needed that. I was already struggling on this road trip, trying to make sure everything went as smoothly as possible. But how could I when I was even having a tough time with drawing—something that had always come so easily before?

"Wait a second, we should—" Cass started.

"We can spare a few days, right?" I asked her. *Please*, I mouthed.

Cass didn't look happy; but she didn't object, either.

7

EUGENE

"Tell me more about this festival," I said to Joaquin as we strolled to the Flynn Rider Museum and Performance Center. Rapunzel, the frog, and Cassandra were on a grand tour led by Abigail from the village council, and Hook Foot and Lance were feasting on sandwiches in a tavern called the Sunshine Cantina. But Joaquin had pulled me aside and asked if he might have a word with me.

"The Flynn Rider Festival is a wonderful chance for our community to come together," Joaquin said. "And you know a thing or two about the literary character we all love so much, don't you?"

"Of course. As an orphan, stories of Flynn Rider gave me courage and heart," I replied.

Joaquin nodded. "When word of Princess Rapunzel's return to Corona reached us—as it did all nearby lands—no one here could believe that her rescuer was the very thief who had been using our hero's name."

"That's me," I said. "Though the truth is, Rapunzel and I rescued each other."

A large body of water came into view. It was unlike any place I'd ever seen! It was swampy, surrounded by low bushes covered with red berries, blanketed in a bluish moss, and scattered with lily pads as big as dinner plates. The air was warmer there, and fresher, too. The scene glimmered under the dappled sunlight. "Is that the Great Bog?" I asked.

"Yes!" Joaquin replied enthusiastically. "Technically it's called Harmony Bog, but it was the Author's inspiration for the Great Bog—which Flynn Rider would cross by swinging from the vines."

"Amazing!"

The closer we got, the more I felt the magic of Harmony Glen that was so perfectly captured in the Flynn Rider stories. The air smelled like flowers and dirt, but in a good way. The plants were lush, and almost junglelike—from what I'd heard about jungles.

"Oh, man, I really want to try that vine!" I said, gazing up at the vine hanging tantalizingly high above the ground.

"Right now?" Joaquin asked.

"Can I?" I asked.

"I suppose it's as good a time as any. To quote the Author, 'Only the now is real.'"

"I don't remember that quote," I said, running through the Flynn Rider stories collected in my mind. "And I thought I knew them all. It reminds me of a similar quote. . . ."

"Oh, mark my words. The Author wrote that," Joaquin replied. "And it's become something of a town motto."

"Wow. You're kind of blowing my mind, Joaquin," I said as I considered his words. I definitely didn't recall the quote, but I couldn't argue with the idea. I was a "live in the moment" kind of guy, too. I couldn't wait to share it with Rapunzel. I repeated his phrase: "Only the now is real."

"So why not take a swing?" Joaquin asked, gesturing to the vine that was hanging from a giant willow. "Legend has it that the Author would often swing a few times before breakfast. Said it helped clear his mind before a day of writing."

"I'll try it!" I said, taking purposeful strides toward a tall tree. I remembered phrases from the books I'd read so many times. Flynn Rider was always swinging around. It had inspired some of my great thieving moves in the past. I was over stealing, but I'd never get over adventure. And as I climbed up the tree I could feel the spirit of adventure in my blood. *Rapunzel will love this*, I thought.

When I got to a high branch, I discovered some wooden panels—perhaps a former tree house. It had to have been the one that the Author had modeled Flynn Rider's perch on! From way up there I could see Rapunzel and Cassandra and an entourage walking the grounds. "Aw, Blondie," I said to myself as I watched her open her notebook and sketch what was probably a flower—or even a ladybug on a flower. She saw the beauty in everything.

Wishing she could see me now, I took hold of the vine, got a grip, and swung! The bog looked amazing from up there—sparkling patches of water amid green sprigs of plants and vibrant wildflowers! And that crazy bright blue moss was everywhere. I spotted a group of kids in the far corner of the bog.

"Helllooooo!" I called as I flew over them. They looked up and waved.

"Hey! Is that Flynn Rider?" one of them exclaimed.

"Nope!" I said. "A visitor! But in my heart, I . . ."

There wasn't much time for conversation. I was almost across!

"Wow!" I said as I landed on the other side of the Great Bog. Because of her hair, Rapunzel was the one who did most of the swinging, but maybe in Harmony Glen we could swing together.

"Bravo," Joaquin said, startling me for a moment.

"That was a dream come true!" I said. "Seriously, I've been wanting to do that since I was a little kid. Hey, speaking of kids . . . I saw a bunch doing something over there."

"Oh, yes, children love to play in the bog. There's so much to discover and explore."

"It was pretty adorable. They thought I was Flynn Rider," I said.

"Oh, yes, why didn't I think of this sooner?" Joaquin said, clapping me on the back. "You should play the role of Flynn Rider in our production."

"Me? An actor? Playing the part I've been study-ing for my entire life? Well, except for the last year. I've been playing a different part. Only that's not a part. That's me. The real me. Eugene."

"The only real is now," Joaquin said. "Come, come."

We started to walk again and reached the Flynn Rider Museum and Performance Center.

"Eugene, I just see that you have a purpose here that is so clear," Joaquin continued as we climbed the steps and entered. We turned to the right and strolled through what seemed to be a backstage area, filled with costumes, painted sets, and props.

"It's just that Flynn Rider is who I pretended to be . . ." I began.

"Think about when you were a boy, reading these stories. How they filled you with joy."

"That's true. They basically saved my life."

"That's the joy that I think you can bring to the festival," Joaquin said. "You'll even get to wear this replica cape."

"*The cape?*" I gasped. The cape was legendary, epic. And it was right in front of me on a costume rack! "But wait—who was playing the part until I arrived? I don't want to take someone else's part away."

"I was," Joaquin said. "But I've got other responsibilities. Besides, you have the youth. And such purpose. It's a job I now see that only you can do."

A job that wasn't dish duty. A purpose. That sounded good to me.

"I wouldn't want to deny the children their inspiration . . ." I said as I fingered the cape, trying it on just for size. I couldn't resist. I reached for the rakish cap that was on display nearby.

"There you are!" Rapunzel said as she walked in with Cass and their tour guide from the village council. Pascal was perched on her shoulder, eyeing a prop frog with curiosity. "Oh, I love the hat!" Rapunzel said to me.

"Thanks," I said.

"If it pleases you, Princess, I've asked Eugene to play the part of Flynn Rider for our festival."

"Very nice," Abigail said.

"The one in a few days?" Cassandra asked.

"Would it really be so bad to stay for a little while in this place?" I asked.

"It *is* beautiful here," Rapunzel said.

"And it would help us out immensely," Joaquin added. "The village council and I are working so hard on a . . . new project for Harmony Glen."

"The town emblem, right?" I asked. "For the sign?"

"That's part of it. And we'd like to unveil it all during the Flynn Rider Festival!"

"Oh, fun! I love new plans! What else will be revealed?" Rapunzel asked.

"I've vowed secrecy so as not to ruin the surprise," Joaquin said. "But all I can say is that your help would allow us to reach our goal."

"We would love to help," Rapunzel said. "And isn't that what so many of the Flynn Rider stories are about? Helping others?"

"Indeed," Joaquin said.

"Then it's settled." Rapunzel beamed.

PART
TWO

HARMONY GLEN

8

CASSANDRA

"We hope you enjoyed our tour. Please make yourselves at home," Abigail said as we exited the Flynn Rider Museum and Performance Center, leaving Fitzherbert to his conversation with Joaquin about rehearsals and when he needed to be "off book."

"We will," Raps said. She'd stopped and sketched every pretty thing that she saw. Butterflies, trees, flowers. Though I wanted to get back on the road, it was good to see her happy. "I can't believe we saw a double rainbow."

"We do seem to have more rainbows than most places," Abigail said. "As you may know, we have our own ecosystem here."

"Any fairies?" I asked. "Unicorns?"

Raps jabbed me in the ribs. She was gentle, but firm.

"I'm still waiting to see a unicorn," Abigail said with a grin. "I haven't given up hope, though!"

Owl soared overhead, careening through the cloudless sky.

"Why does Harmony Glen have its own ecosystem?" Raps asked.

"Because of the bog," Abigail answered. "The blue moss growing there is so packed with nutrients it has special properties. It allows for all these unique flowers to grow. It actually breathes, creating a protective canopy that allows us to have our own weather and unique species, like these three-winged butterflies. It's precious, and as far as we know, it only exists here."

"That's amazing!" Raps said.

"Only here?" I asked. Abigail nodded. Raps and I would have to check out this bog so I could add it to my maps. Anything one-of-a-kind had to be included.

"Some say that when the Author wrote about protecting the gold of Harmony Glen, he really was writing about our blue moss," Abigail added.

"I can't wait to tell Eugene," Raps said. "He's really into the bog."

An older man with gray hair crossed our path. He was walking a horse.

"Hi there," Raps said. "May I pet your horse?" He nodded in response, and Raps gently stroked the horse's nose. "Aw, she's so sweet. Her eyes are full of love."

The man nodded again before moving on.

"That's quiet Edmond," Abigail said. "Doesn't say much, but he's a kind soul."

"Where did Max and Fidella go?" I asked when Edmond and his horse had passed.

"To the stables," Abigail said. "I hope you don't mind. Martina took them there for grooming and a fine lunch of fresh hay, ripe juicy apples, and carrots so plump and sweet you could eat them for dessert."

My stomach started to rumble. Raps laughed, and then Abigail did, too.

"What?" I said. "I'm hungry."

"Then I have to take you to the Sunshine Cantina," Abigail said. She gestured to a sign above that pointed south and read SUNSHINE CANTINA. "It's the best food here. Fit for a princess and a lady-in-waiting. On the menu today is a vegetable soufflé, a garden salad, homemade brown bread with freshly churned butter, and banana cream pie for dessert, which I have a feeling you'll love."

"Banana cream pie is Cass's favorite!" Raps said.

"Shhh," I said. She'd discovered that one night back at the castle. Raps made me every dessert she could think of until she was convinced she'd found my favorite. I was never really a dessert person, but banana cream pie was something I could just never turn down. Still, I didn't need anyone else to have that information.

"How'd *you* know that?" I asked Abigail.

"Who doesn't love banana cream pie?" Abigail said. She had a point. "Come on, let's go get some food!"

Raps linked her arm in mine and we headed in the direction of lunch.

"What exactly are we going to do here for a few days?" I asked Raps as we followed Abigail down a wooden pathway.

"Help out," Raps said with a shrug. "I know this means the world to Eugene. And you did say you wanted some extra time to work on your maps. When she mentioned the bog, I knew you were going to want to add it."

"I assure you, you will not be bored in Harmony Glen," Joaquin said, seeming to appear out of nowhere.

Raps and I both jumped a little.

"You sure are light on your feet," I said.

Joaquin gave me a quick smile and kept walking. "We have an archery field that I think you'll enjoy. And we have art classes, too. Perhaps you'd like to join one of them this afternoon, Rapunzel?"

"I'd love that," Raps said as we stepped inside the Sunshine Cantina, which was exactly what it sounded like—a large, open-air tent with low tables and comfortable cushions for sitting on. Colorful tapestries decorated the walls.

The table was definitely set to perfection. It would pass my lady-in-waiting test any day of the week. Everything was crisp and clean, and there were even purple flowers on all the tables. I was about to complain that there wasn't any food when a steaming loaf of bread was placed in front of me. It was so warm that the butter melted as soon as it touched the bread, and a tall glass of lavender lemonade was poured from a crystal pitcher into a goblet.

"We will leave you ladies to enjoy this meal while we return to the leadership pavilion," Joaquin said. "It may seem like all we do is have fun around here, but there is work to be done. Mark my words!"

"If there's anything you need, please come and find us," Abigail said. "Just follow the signs. . . ."

Raps and I nodded. We both ate hungrily. It was wonderful to have a hot meal after being on the road.

"Okay, fine," I said, wiping my mouth, once we were finished with lunch. "I admit it. That was good."

"It really was. I am satisfied, but not overly full," Raps said. "They seem to do everything just perfectly here."

"It's kind of weird, right?" I asked.

"Let's give them a chance," Raps said. "Oh, that must be the art class over there."

She pointed to a group of people working with easels. They were all painting the same view: pretty hills covered in waving wildflowers.

"Are you going to join them?" I asked.

"I think I'd rather explore, and maybe work on my portrait a bit. Are you okay finding the archery fields?" she asked.

"I'm pretty sure I can find them," I said, pointing to those signs with the gold letters that were everywhere. "Just follow the signs. Not too difficult."

"I'll see you for dinner," Raps said, giving me a quick hug.

I started to follow the signs to the sporting fields, but then decided I'd take a detour. I wanted a closer look at this "amazing" bog. It wasn't difficult to find, but it *was* unusual. I'd never seen so many different kinds of plants growing in one place. The weirdest part was the blue moss that covered the water and grew on nearby rocks and logs. It wasn't beautiful like the lagoon that Raps and I had discovered in Corona, but it was definitely a map-worthy location. And the air did feel different—more humid. I took off my boots and dipped a toe into the cool water. I had a small blister from my boots, and I wanted to test the bog's healing abilities. "Ouch." It stung for a moment, but when I removed my foot, the wound *had* closed. So it wasn't just a legend. These waters were healing.

I heard rustling in the distance and hid behind a tree.

There was Joaquin, collecting moss in a jar. My instinct told me to stay concealed. When he'd finished his task, Joaquin looked up, seeming to check for other people. Huh. That was odd. It was almost like he didn't want to be caught taking the moss. Then, just as quickly as he'd appeared, Joaquin slipped away. I lifted my head, discreetly trying to get a better look. But, strangely, I didn't see him take a path. He had seemed to descend into the bog itself.

After a few minutes, once I was sure he was

completely out of sight, I checked out where he'd been. There was no trace of him. *There must be a narrow path that's escaping me*, I thought. After all, it was swampy there, and footsteps could easily disappear.

I shook my head, wondering if the thick bog air was making me loopy.

There was a youngish guy shooting arrows when I arrived at the sporting fields soon after my detour to the bog.

"Hi there," he said after landing a bull's-eye. "My name's Wolf. You must be Cassandra. Want to shoot?"

I nodded. "How'd you know my name?" I asked as the man handed me a tightly strung bow.

"We don't get too many visitors around here," he said. "Word travels fast when we do—especially royalty. And anyway, you're obviously not Rapunzel." He gestured to my short hair.

"You don't get visitors because the town isn't on modern maps," I said, loading my arrow and taking aim at the target.

"We like our peace here," Wolf said as I drew back my bow. "Does wonders for focus."

I released my arrow.

"BAM!" I said. "Bull's-eye!"

"Nice going. Right in the pinhole," Wolf said, and handed me another arrow.

That afternoon I beat my average, hitting more bull's-eyes than ever before. Maybe it was the vegetable soufflé or that darned delicious banana cream pie, but I was on a roll. Or was it that the breeze seemed to be blowing in just the right direction. I wasn't sure. All I knew was I felt more clearheaded and relaxed than I had since we'd started our journey. Maybe there *was* something focusing about this place.

At the end of the afternoon, I stopped by the stables to see Max and Fidella groomed to perfection, swishing their tales in the breeze.

"Well, I guess you guys are good here. . . ." I said. I looked around the peaceful stables. It was still too early for dinner, and the others were preoccupied with their own activities. It seemed I finally had some free time on my hands. "I think I'll go work on my maps and polish the itinerary for the rest of our journey."

Fidella whinnied in response.

Huh. Maybe I could try going with the flow more often.

Maybe perfect wasn't so bad.

9

RAPUNZEL

The afternoon was as sweet as it was warm. I don't think I've ever experienced such delightful weather. I made some sketches as Pascal and I wandered through the village: a flower with what looked to be a million petals, a lilac bush so fragrant I could smell it a hundred paces away, a swallow with a song so catchy I almost sang along, and a whole swarm of three-winged butterflies. Pascal walked along next to me, beaming with joy. He posed playfully for a few of my drawings.

At last I decided to get to work on my self-portrait. I found a structure with a clean window and studied myself in the reflection. Maybe the reason I couldn't draw myself was because I hadn't had a good point of reference.

But then again, I'd never had a problem painting myself before. The portrait I'd drawn for the great hall of my mom and me had captured the warmth I felt toward her.

Mom, I thought, and took a deep breath. I really missed her. She brought me so much comfort, and more than that, courage. If anyone could steer me in the right direction, she could, and for a moment I felt the lack of her. Even though we'd lived apart for almost my whole life, after we'd been reunited, Mom always knew exactly what to say. I wondered, what would she say to me right now?

Sadly, I wasn't sure. I planted my bare feet on the earth. I'd never liked shoes because they stopped me from feeling the ground with my own skin, and allowing myself to bloom wherever I stood.

It's just a self-portrait, I told myself. *Just relax and draw. Drawing is what you've always known, and what you still know now.* I closed my eyes, took a deep breath, and opened them again. I looked at myself in the glass and drew without glancing at the paper.

When I glanced down I saw a mess. My smile was too big. My eyes were too wide. I looked terribly . . . surprised?

"What do you think, Pascal?" I asked. He nodded

and smiled. "Come on, Pascal. Be honest." His face fell. "I know. It's terrible."

Pascal shrugged, sticking out his tongue in a way that made me laugh. I drew him in a flash. He pointed, lighting up.

"I know. I can draw other people. I just don't seem to be able to see myself right now." I thought about that, trying to get to the heart of the matter. For years I had been Rapunzel, the girl raised in the tower, and more recently I'd been Rapunzel, the princess of Corona. But who was I out here? Those things, and . . . ? Pascal did a cute dance and I laughed again. He was right. It was time for me to lighten up. "Yes, let's take a break. What is this place anyway?" He pointed to the signs.

"We're back at the leadership pavilion," I said. "This must just be the back side of it. Let's go take a look."

I poked my head inside. The place was gigantic!

The walls were decorated with the most beautiful tiles. Each of them looked to be individually made and designed—and they all seemed to feature Flynn Rider. I couldn't help giggling at one that depicted Flynn tackling several heroes at once in a giant leap from his rope swing. It was exactly as Eugene had described it.

I heard voices and took a few steps down the hallway, toward the sound.

"I'm just not sure that's right," a female voice said. "The bog is thriving, and we all know it's a delicate ecosystem. Disrupting it is a risk."

I took a daring step closer, toward a large staircase. I was silent, but I didn't notice the mirror on the ceiling, which gave me away.

"Rapunzel?" Joaquin asked. He was sitting at a table with some of the other members of the village council.

"Oh, um, hello," I said with a bashful smile. "I'm so very sorry to intrude. It's just that this hall and staircase are so beautiful. The tiles are exquisite!"

"Yes!" Joaquin's smile was so broad and charming (almost as charming as Eugene's—but not quite). He drew so much attention, as though a spotlight were shining on him, that it nearly distracted me from Abigail's face.

She stood several paces behind him. Her expression was distraught, her features ill arranged. I might not have been able to capture my own expression, but I could recognize pure emotion when I saw it. She was scared.

"Abigail," I said, walking toward her. "Are you okay?"

The expression vanished as quickly as it had appeared.

"Abigail?" Joaquin asked, his own face filled with concern. "What's wrong?"

"Nothing!" Abigail said. She tapped her chest with her hand and took a sip of water. "Wrong pipe."

"I'm so glad you appreciate our art," Joaquin said, whisking me to the other side of the room. I noticed a giant mural of the village showing all the villagers holding hands. "Here is our most beautiful example. It gets to the heart of the village council. Would anyone care to explain it to the princess?"

"Let me," said Abigail, dabbing her lips with her napkin and standing up. "The village council formed after the great storm, when there was great chaos."

"Oh, yes, the storm!" I said. "We heard something about that. . . ."

"Before the storm there were no true leaders, and this fair land was overrun with crime and debauchery," Joaquin said. "And, of course, when the weather raged, there were no emergency systems in place."

"The light of Harmony Glen was nearly put out," Abigail continued. "But Joaquin and others stepped up and established order and peace, and created a system to ensure that all of our inhabitants would remain safe and happy, in our own little slice of paradise."

"Wow," I said, impressed. I had started learning about what went into running a kingdom in the past year, and of course, I had found it pretty tricky to make the right judgment calls just in the caravan the past few days; it was no easy feat to lead.

"I've just had the most marvelous idea," Joaquin said. "Would you help the art students create a new mural for the festival? Perhaps right on the inside of the border wall? Something full of happiness!"

"I'd love to," I said. "A series of self-portraits, created by the people. How lovely!"

Martina motioned for me to join them at the table and then brought me a cup of tea and a slice of cake. As Abigail continued, elaborating on the many joys of Harmony Glen, I wondered if I'd only imagined that look of distress and the crease across her brow, of which now there was no trace.

10

EUGENE

"'Ride on, fellow bandits of bravery!'" I said, drawing myself up tall and facing the empty auditorium as I read the last line of the script. I gestured broadly, just as the script indicated. "'May your goodness spread like peanut butter on warm bread, fresh from the ovens of brotherhood. . . .'" I flashed my most charming smile and then turned to our director and playwright, Alfonso. "Um, 'ovens of brotherhood'?" I knew he was a member of the village council, and I didn't want to offend him. And yet, as an actor, the *lead* actor no less, I had a duty to interpret the words I spoke with meaning and understanding. I smiled as I stroked my goatee in a most theatrical manner. "Is that a . . . *necessary* line?"

Alfonso nodded immediately, as though he hadn't even considered my point.

"Oh, come on!" I said, playfully punching him in the arm. *Ovens of brotherhood?* It was awful! I'd be embarrassed to utter it in front of Rapunzel. And if Cass heard it she'd never let me live it down. "Do you think we could replace this with one of the Author's more famous lines? You know, a classic Flynnigan phrase like, 'Tallyho, though courage be invisible in idea, in action it exists in plain sight! Let us paint the world with it!'"

"I don't know that one," Alfonso said.

"Whaaaaat?" I asked. "I engraved it on the wall of the orphanage!"

"Excuse me, but we are in Harmony Glen, home of the Author, and I'm an expert on his work. If I don't know that line, then it was ne'er writ," Alfonso said.

Ne'er writ? Oh, boy.

"I mean, no offense," he continued.

"Offense taken!" I said. I was the lead, after all!

Alfonso sighed. "Eugene, go have a look in our library. If you can find that sentence, I'll put it in the play."

Excellent. I'd be waxing poetic with Rider's best lines in no time.

"Deal!" I replied, and we shook on it.

"But for now, please stick to the script," Alfonso added, peering at me from under his heavy black-rimmed glasses. "Bread is the very sustenance of life, and peanut butter is the only condiment of nutritional value. It's a great line. It may be . . . immortal."

"Oh," I said. "Right. Okay, we'll do it that way for now."

I glanced at my fellow castmates, who now included Hook Foot as a three-winged butterfly with several dance solos, and Lance.

Hook Foot was thrilled to show off the moves he'd practiced his whole life. When Alfonso had cast him, Hook Foot proclaimed it was a dream come true. He even had a solo.

"Perfect," Alfonso had said. He'd needed a soprano who could dance to round out the cast.

"I confess I'm not immune to the acting bug," Lance had added, having been listening in.

"Then be Townsperson Number Four," Alfonso replied. "To be honest, I don't even need another townsperson, but if it'll make you—"

"It will be my honor," Lance had said, bowing as though he were before royalty. "I serve language; I serve art; I will tread the boards with dignity and grace."

"Huh?" I asked.

"Dude, I've always wanted to act," he said.

"You have?"

He nodded, and then he bowed again. I guess the stage has a way of taking people over. For the rest of the rehearsal, Lance threw himself into the role of Townsperson Number Four as though it had been written by the greatest bard ever to live. And his only lines were: "Yes!" "Oh, dear!" and "That cannot be!"

Now a familiar voice interrupted us. "Is this where rehearsal is?"

"Cass?" I'd encouraged her to join us in the production earlier, but I'd never imagined that she actually would.

"I'm here," she said, crossing her arms. Her posture said *I'm perturbed* but her eyes shone.

"I wasn't planning on coming, but I don't know. After shooting several bull's-eyes in a row, I guess I'm in a good mood," she said, and then turned to Alfonso. "So what do you need me to be?"

Jeez. I guess everyone thinks they can act!

Alfonso tapped his chin as he surveyed the group in front of him. At last he spoke. "I need a tree."

I tried to stifle a laugh. Cass glared.

"Dust allergy," I said, trying to explain my fake laugh-sneeze. "You were saying, Alfonso?"

"I could use Cassandra as a tree," he said.

"Are you kidding me?" Cass asked.

I bit my lip so that I wouldn't laugh louder. I tried to think grim thoughts. That wasn't easy. I had to go really dark.

"I kid you not!" Alfonso said. "This is no small part! You must plant your roots in the earth and eat up the nutrients."

He bent his knees and inhaled deeply.

Cass curled her lip and eyed him skeptically. "Excuse me?"

"You are a tree. Is there any greater warrior than one who can ground in the earth and sway with the wind?" Alfonso asked. Cass raised an eyebrow. "Don't you see? Your strength is in your deeply held beliefs, which give you the flexibility to adjust to different circumstances and to reach for greatness! I sense your doubt, but join me, here on the stage. As an actor, it is your job to find the truth in the role. It is your job to be—a tree."

Cass squinted thoughtfully. "I suppose trees are important."

Well, look who was finally loosening up!

"Without a doubt," Alfonso said. "We may not

notice them or appreciate them every day, but if they were to disappear, our lives would be so much poorer."

"You know, you have a point," Cass said.

I glanced down at my shoes. I didn't want to make eye contact with Cass, because I was witnessing one of the rarest phenomena on earth—Cass was smiling! She was following Alfonso's lead! This place was magic. It had to be!

Hook Foot started practicing his solo, singing with all his heart: *"When the path is blocked, find your wings, and fly, fly, fly."*

I took a deep breath and resolved to say my peanut butter line with the conviction of none other than Flynn Rider. . . .

Temporarily, of course. I'd still search the library later.

11

RAPUNZEL

"What I like to do when I'm painting the sunset is to blend the colors with my thumb, like this," I said to Abigail, demonstrating the technique in my notebook with a delicate touch.

It was a relief to be talking about art—something familiar. Being out on the road and experiencing so many new challenges was not all "folk dancin' and fricassee frog legs," as Pearly had said.

Abigail smiled as she tried my method. She'd told me emphatically that she wasn't an artist, but when I had mentioned to her back in the pavilion how much I loved creating art, she'd gamely taken a notebook and a fresh set of pastels from the sweet little art supply shed and led me to a look-out point that was, uncharacteristically, devoid of signs. Even though we had lingered over the chamomile tea and lavender pound cake, it sort of felt like she'd wanted to get me out of the village council's meeting quickly for some reason. Joaquin had had a quick word with Abigail, and as soon as I'd finished, she'd whisked me away.

Now I watched a smile spread over her face. "It's lovely just how many colors get created, isn't it?" I asked.

"It's really satisfying," she said. "Even though art is definitely not my talent—I'm enjoying it!"

I could tell she meant it. Her brown eyes were sparkling with flecks of green and gold, and the crease that had divided her brow earlier was gone completely. I realized then that even though she was a member of the village council, Abigail couldn't have been much older than I was.

"I've never really understood the word 'talent,'" I said, vocalizing the thought for the first time. "I mean, I guess there are things we happen to be better at naturally—or maybe there are subjects that we are just more interested in—but I don't believe we were born just for one task. We can thrive doing lots of things."

"What do you mean, Princess?" Abigail asked.

She was using my blending technique liberally— so much so that her background was turning a bit dark. But as the sun set, the sky did darken, so who was I to judge?

"I guess I'm thinking about my role as princess, and how if I were to truly be the best princess I could be, I couldn't put any labels on myself," I said. "I like to think I'm not only a princess. I'm also an artist, a warrior, an explorer, and a friend."

"Hmmm . . ." Abigail said. There was a blue smudge on her cheek that made me laugh. "What?"

"Nothing," I said, wiping her cheek with my handkerchief. "Just a little bit of blue." She laughed, and at last her youth shone through.

"Here's what I think about talent," I said. "If you're really curious about something, if in your heart you want to know all about a subject—whatever it is: painting, acting, archery, swordsmanship—then your heart and mind will inevitably compel you to discover it. Lift every stone! Examine each leaf! And before you know it, you'll have a talent."

Abigail showed me her picture of the sunset. She was beaming, and in a moment, I realized what her expression reminded me of. She was looking at her work like I looked at Eugene. She had accomplished what every great artist must, in my opinion— channeling emotion and love into her painting.

"Do you have a sweetheart, Abigail?" I asked. Her face paled. "I'm sorry. I didn't mean to upset you."

"It's okay," she said. "I did have a sweetheart once. But he no longer . . . he . . . I'd rather not talk about it."

"I understand," I said.

Just then, a chorus of bells rang out through the hills.

"What is that?" I asked, dusting off my dress and standing up.

"It's the call for Evensing!" she said. Once again, her face broke into a gigantic smile. "Come."

"What is that?" I asked.

"You'll see."

We gathered our art supplies, putting our pastels and paintbrushes in our pockets. Abigail took my hand, leading me through some thick brush, until at last we were on a path to the town wall.

The closer we got, the louder the bells rang in harmony.

In the distance I heard a rhythmic beat. "Abigail, what is that music?"

"The Evensing!" Abigail said, leading me quickly down the path to a clearing with a large wall surrounding it, much like the one that marked the border of Corona.

"Look," she said.

All the townspeople were line dancing! Everyone knew the moves and the music. There was a group of musicians playing a jaunty rhythm and—I swear it looked like magic—the entire town was going along with it.

"This is so . . . creative!" I said to Abigail. Or at least I thought I had. She had joined the group so seamlessly that I hadn't even realized when she'd left my side.

The entire town was there, either singing or dancing or playing an instrument.

Cass, of course, was sitting on the sidelines, evaluating everything. I laughed as I watched Eugene, Lance, and Hook Foot join in the dance.

I was so glad Eugene had suggested we come here. From my afternoon art lesson with Abigail to this village dance, I felt so inspired! I decided to join the musicians onstage.

"Hello! My name is Rapunzel," I said to one of the musicians, who appeared to be taking a break. She had gray hair and lines around her eyes.

"I know," she answered, smiling warmly. "I'm Carole."

"You sound amazing, Carole! Are you by any chance taking a break?" I asked. She nodded. "Is there any way I could, um, borrow that?" I pointed to her guitar.

"Of course," she said, handing me her instrument.

"Thank you so, so much," I said, taking the guitar.

I patiently waited for the song to end and then said as loudly as I could, "Thank you so much for welcoming us! And here's a Rapunzel original!"

12

CASSANDRA

I might have agreed to be a tree earlier, but I hadn't let my guard down completely. So I understood exactly what was happening when Raps started to improvise on the guitar. Everyone stopped doing their weird dance and looked in our direction as though we had just fired a cannonball. A group of older people wore expressions of confusion. A gray-haired woman wrung her hands. A teenage boy had a glimmer in his eye, even though his face remained calm.

"Not feeling it?" Raps asked the group. "It was a little too down tempo, maybe. Don't worry, I can kick it up a notch!"

Something odd was going on, but it wasn't about

the tempo. Knowing Raps, she probably thought she needed to infuse more love and passion into her act in order to get a response. She couldn't assess the situation from up on stage, but from down where I was, I could feel the tension in the air.

"This is one of my favorite tunes," she said. "And I hope that you'll like it, too."

She closed her eyes and mustered up more enthusiasm than I'd thought was humanly possible. Then she dashed to the front of the stage and belted out her song with gusto.

I looked for Eugene, who was so in love with Rapunzel he was cheering her on—but he was the only one.

It was kind of hard to watch. I waved my arms to give her a signal.

That's when I saw Joaquin walking toward the stage, taking purposeful strides. He had a placid look on his face like always, but his jaw was tight. I spotted a back entrance to the stage and made a run for it.

"So that's not a hit, either?" Raps was asking the crowd as I dashed toward her. She continued, "Well, don't worry, I know a lot of different songs and I—"

"Raps!" I called from the wings.

She paused, and I gestured for her to come over,

but she only looked confused. Then I went to her, took her by the hand, and led her down the stairs. Sometimes all those years in the tower really showed.

"If I tried some of my other pieces, I think they would have liked it. They just seemed slow to warm up, you know?" Raps said. The song that the band had been playing before Raps jumped onstage once again filled the streets. "Hey, where are we going in such a rush?"

"Raps, they were looking at you like you were nuts," I said. I didn't know how else to break it to her. She was already struggling with her painting, and I didn't want her to start having issues with music, too. But something wasn't right. When we ran into Joaquin, my bad feeling grew worse.

"Creativity is a beautiful thing," Joaquin pronounced.

"I feel the same way," Rapunzel said. "Though I guess I wasn't striking the right, er, note?"

"Please don't take any offense," Joaquin said. "It's just that the people of Harmony Glen prefer familiar songs."

"That must get boring," I said. Raps nudged me.

"On the contrary, it's comforting. There's just enough change to keep people on their feet and achieve a sense of mastery."

"Huh?" I said.

"I'm not sure I follow, either," Raps said. "But I apologize. We *are* guests here." She squeezed my hand as she said this. "And we need to follow your customs."

"Your Highness," Joaquin said, bowing, "your royal blood is evident in your innate understanding of gentility."

"She's just being . . . Raps," I said. Because if he thought I wasn't picking up on the subtext—that I was not demonstrating gentility—he was mistaken. I was about to inform him that a lot more goes into being royal than just gentility, when Eugene rushed to our sides.

"Everything okay over here?" Eugene asked.

"It's fine," I said.

"I could feel your testiness from across the courtyard, Cass," Eugene said.

A bugle sounded, interrupting our conversation. The townspeople gathered and hushed. They watched en masse as from atop the giant wall, a huge scroll was unfurled. It seemed to have the names of everyone in the village on it.

"What is that?" I said.

"Cass," Rapunzel said, urging me to quiet down.

"That's quite a, um, er, roster you've got there," Eugene said.

"Look how excited they are," Joaquin said, gesturing to the people, who were gathering closer to the scroll. "How filled with anticipation."

"What, um, exactly is that?" Raps asked.

"Is it a score card?" I asked, taking note of the stars. "Is there a contest going on?"

"Sort of," Joaquin said.

The village council stood on the stage.

"It was a wonderful Evensing," Joaquin said.

I noticed Wolf, the guy from the archery field, sitting nearby. I beckoned him over.

"Hey, Wolf," I said. "What is this?"

"It's the star chart," he said. "Everyone is awarded stars based on how much they contributed to the greater good of the community. It's all about coming together and helping one another."

"That's nice," Rapunzel said. "I think."

"Hmm," I said, not sure if this was adding up. Who was defining the greater good?

"With the arrival of our luminous guests, we have some new stars today!" Joaquin said. "And as a welcoming symbol, I'd like to give honorary stars to Rapunzel, and Eugene, Cassandra, Lance, and Hook Foot. We don't have many visitors, and we are so lucky that these fine Coronans, including the princess herself, chose to come and see us."

"If you were on the map, you'd get more visitors,"

I said, voicing my thoughts more loudly than I'd intended.

"I told you, keeping to ourselves is how everything stays so calm around here," Wolf said. "Haven't you ever heard stories of villagers in beautiful places messing up signs so that tourists leave them alone?"

"I guess so. . . ." I said.

"But visitors can be peaceful. And they can also bring in new ideas and new songs," Rapunzel said.

"It's just easier," Wolf said. He looked around. "You know, I think I'm needed over there."

"But don't you think that when you keep everyone out, that . . . Hey, Wolf?" I called to him, but he slipped away into the crowd before I could finish my point.

13

EUGENE

I'd never slept so well as that first night in Harmony Glen. Maybe it was the gentle evening breezes, or the way the body relaxes after a good day of exercise and fun, or how at ease I was in the company of so many other Flynn Rider fans, but I woke up the next day bright and early with a hop in my step. My hair looked great, too. I peered out the caravan window, where I saw Rapunzel sitting on a rock, drawing. She must have slept as well as I had to be up so early and already working on her art. Maybe Harmony Glen was helping her artist's block.

At the same moment I had that thought, she huffed with frustration, erased a line, and tried again. I wished there was something I could do to help her realize that whatever she was dealing with would pass, that she could start a new drawing instead. But she was so determined with this self-portrait that I didn't think she would want that particular advice. Maybe I could distract her instead!

"Where are you going, Casanova?" Cass asked me, pulling me back by my shirt. Had she been just waiting there outside the caravan door, ready to attack?

"First I was going to go say good morning to my girlfriend, and then I was going to do some research at the Flynn Rider Library, and following that intellectual endeavor, I was going to stretch and warm up my vocal chords before rehearsal," I said. "Have you forgotten that I'm the lead in the play?"

"I doubt you'd ever let me do that," Cass said.

Be kind, I thought, stopping myself from a wonderfully sharp retort. *Rapunzel wants us to get along.*

"You should join me," I suggested. "I've heard the library is great. And you're in the play, too."

"Aye, 'tis a good lass who is prepared for a hard day's work," Lance said, appearing behind me in his costume. He'd insisted on taking it home the night before.

"'Aye'?" Cass echoed, arching an eyebrow the way she often did.

"Aye," Lance repeated.

"He's in character," I explained.

"As Townsperson Number Four?" she asked.

"That's his part!" I said.

"Does the good lady take issue with that?" Lance asked. "My name is Thomas, by the way."

"Whatever floats your boat," Cass said, shaking it off.

"There's no need to get sarcastic," I said. I gestured to the rolling hills around us. "Especially here. Isn't this place working on you just a teeny tiny bit?"

Me, me, me, me . . ." I heard Hook Foot practicing his scales inside the caravan. He had a surprisingly good singing voice.

"A falsetto," Cass mused. "Who knew?"

"That's the spirit! Just relax, enjoy, and be a happy tree. It's fun!" I took her by the shoulders. "Do you even know what that is?"

"Hands off, Fitzherbert," she said. "Of course I know what fun is, it's just that I have this little thing I have to do called protecting the princess and saving the kingdom. It's my job—oh, wait, do you even know what that is?"

"That *almost* hurt," I said, scowling.

"Are you two fighting?" Rapunzel asked, apparently abandoning her art.

"Good morning, Blondie," I said, giving her a hug.

"Hi, Eugene," she answered. The smolder was working! Aha! She softened. "What are you doing today?" she asked.

"I was innocently about to come say hi when I was accosted by Cass. 'Luckily it is not with me, as it is with those whom small things dismay'—Flynn Rider quote, by the way. And then I was going to go to do some research and go to rehearsal with my fellow actors."

"Actors? I am but a townsperson. A pheasant minder, if you must know," Lance said.

"Pheasant minder?" I asked. "Is that a thing?"

"I mind the pheasants," Lance said. He broke character for a moment as he explained. "In the time period that Flynn Rider lived in it was a popular occupation. I think it suits Townsperson Number Four. I mean, Thomas."

"Out of all the professions . . ." I began, but noticing the look on Lance's face I changed direction and clapped him on the shoulder. "You know what, buddy? Never mind. I think that's great—"

"Look, enough about the play. We need to leave, Rapunzel," Cass said impatiently. "This place gives me the creeps. Besides, we should get going any-way to make our first *planned* stop."

"Cassandra, you are just so unaccustomed to happiness that I think you're confused," I said. I didn't get the sense that we were in danger.

"You know, I'm with Cass on this one. That whole chart of stars did kind of throw me off. . . ." Rapunzel said.

"Really?" I asked.

"I'm not saying that I think we need to leave or make any sudden decisions, but it was kinda weird," Rapunzel said.

"But the chart is just stars on paper. It's hardly an arsenal of weapons. Like *some* people like to carry around," I said.

"When you're the daughter of the captain of the guard, you naturally build up a collection. Kind of like you have six different hairbrushes?"

"Three are for facial hair," I said. "Why do I even bother defending myself? Their festival is in a few short days. They need a lead in the play. . . ."

"And a three-winged butterfly," Hook Foot said, "with a graceful dance guaranteed to enchant!"

"And a pheasant minder," Lance said.

At that moment three of the actual townspeople, including Daphne, the sweet child with the big dimples, approached us. She carried a basket of muffins. Another girl who had to be her twin carried a basket of fresh fruit, and a third girl brought a pitcher of fresh milk. They also had what looked like spades in their pockets.

"We brought you some breakfast," Daphne said. "These are my sisters, Molly and Grace, and we wanted to show our gratitude and hospitality."

"Thank you," Rapunzel said as we all helped ourselves to muffins, fruit, and milk. "This is just so sweet!"

"And Mr. Fitzherbert . . ." Molly said.

"Call me Eugene," I said.

"You really do look just like I've always imagined Flynn Rider to," Molly said.

"When I grow up, I want to be just like you," Grace said. "Brave and true to your word."

"Thanks, kiddo," I said. "Are those little shovels you guys are carrying?"

"Yes," Molly said, taking hers out to display it. "Joaquin gave them to us as gifts."

"I guess everyone has their own idea of what makes a good present," Cass said.

"They're supposed to symbolize the wholesome hard work that makes Harmony Glen so great," Daphne added.

"There's going to be a shovel parade on Flynn Rider Day," Grace said.

"A shovel parade?" Cass said. "That's just bizarre."

"To each his own," Rapunzel said. "Maybe our customs would seem odd to them."

"Rapunzel, we hear *you* are a great artist," Grace said, turning her attention to Rapunzel. "We hope you join our art class today by the lookout."

"Absolutely!" Rapunzel said.

Then the children scampered off.

"You heard the kids—I have to stay brave and true to my word," I said. "Cassandra, it's only two more days. Can't you just . . . be a tree?"

Cassandra sighed, clearly overruled. "I guess so. But I'll be keeping my eyes open. And no matter what anyone says, I'm not going to any shovel parade."

"Wonderful!" I said. "I'm so glad that's settled. Now, I have to go to the library before rehearsal starts or else I'm going to be stuck with a line about peanut butter that is *really* taking me out of the moment. Anyone want to come with?"

"I'm up for some research," Cass said.

"I knew you'd get into this, Cassandra," I said, pleasantly surprised. Finally, we were getting somewhere this morning. "Imagine: Cassandra reading Flynn Rider in her free time. If there was ever any proof that the magic of Harmony Glen is real, I think we have it."

"I'm interested in the maps, Fitzherbert," she said. "And when exactly this place was removed from them."

"Hey, I'll take it," I said. "Blondie? Are you in?"

"Absolutely," she said. "Would I ever say no to a library?"

The Flynn Rider Library was a small wooden cabin with a fireplace, a comfy rug, comfortable chairs and, of course, books! If I had ever pictured a perfect reading nook, this was it.

"Pretty great, right, ladies?" I asked as I opened the drapes and light flooded the room.

"There have to be some old maps in here," Cassandra said.

"It's so cozy and woodsy!" Rapunzel said, testing out an inviting sofa. "I just love a room full of books, no matter how small."

"Aw, Blondie. When you talk about libraries your mouth does this cute little smiley thing on one side that is just beyond adorable," I said, falling even more in love with her.

"Eugene, you are the sweetest," she replied.

"Bingo!" Cassandra said, reaching past us and pulling down a thick volume covered in a layer of dust. "An atlas!"

"Oh, let's see!" Rapunzel said as Cassandra took a seat next to her on the sofa.

I started searching the stacks. "I'd better find that quote I'm looking for. Poor old Alfonso doesn't understand who he's messing with," I said, running a finger across the different spines. "I know exactly the story it's in: *Flynnigan Rider and the Journey to Zamora*. Aha! Here it is. Now to find chapter eighteen!" I plucked the volume from the shelves and began to thumb through it.

"This is missing pages," Cassandra said.

"She's right," Rapunzel said. "I see the surrounding area, including the spot where Grandma Pearl's roadside stand is . . ."

"But there's no Harmony Glen—in the atlas in the town library," Cassandra added.

I stared at the book in my hand, realization dawning on me. "There are pages missing here, too," I said. "All of chapter eighteen is gone—and it's the best one in the book, the carnival of Zamora. The way the Author describes the masks is so transporting! This is a crime. Removing chapter eighteen is a felony, at the very least. I bet it was Alfonso. He got here before me and—"

"Eugene, look. Sentences in other books are blacked out," Rapunzel said, holding out another book.

"What?" I asked, rushing toward her. "From *Flynn Rider and the Band of Ragged Travelers*? That's insane. This more than any other book is the one that made me want to seek out new experiences. That Alfonso is thorough!"

"This might not just be about the play," Rapunzel said gently.

"I have a feeling this goes beyond a line about peanut butter," Cass added.

"Point taken. But there has to be a good explanation," I said.

"Like what?" Cassandra asked.

In a very rare moment, I found myself speechless.

14

RAPUNZEL

We each left the library a little more unsettled. Cass was now more convinced than ever that something was really off about this place. She wanted to leave—she said she had enough information for her maps. Eugene seemed shaken by the pages and passages that had been removed from tons of the books in the library, but he was also sure there had to be a reason. As I set out with my paints and easel toward where the children had said the art class would be, I felt more torn than ever.

My destiny was looming before me. I knew that we needed to follow the rocks and save the kingdom. At the same time, another part of my journey was getting to know the world I'd ached to see for so long, and getting to know the people in it. Being there in Harmony Glen was part of the experience I had been craving. I didn't want to abandon it out of fear because of some missing maps and odd customs. And I admired that Eugene wanted to keep his promise to be in the play. The way those girls looked up to him was so sweet. I loved that he didn't want to let them down.

I stifled a yawn. I'd woken up early to work on my self-portrait, but I didn't seem to be getting any closer to my vision. Every time I attempted to make my painting better, I seemed to make it worse! Hopefully, a day with fellow artists would inspire me. And if Cass could just hang in there a little longer, maybe we'd all leave full of Flynn Rider's spirit. At least, that's what I told myself. Or was I just not ready to be out on the road again?

I had just spotted the art class when someone behind me said, "Would you like me to help you with those supplies?"

I turned to see Wolf, the young man who had been talking with Cass the night before at Evensing. He was smiling and offering a helping hand.

"That would actually be great," I said, handing him the easel. "We didn't officially meet, but I'm Rapunzel."

"I know," he said with a kind smile. "Everyone knows who you are. I'm Wolf. I'm a member of the welcoming committee."

"I remember you from last night," I said as we walked along the well-marked path toward the scenic overlook. "You know my friend Cass."

"She and I shot some arrows yesterday," he said. "She's so good with a bow."

"She really is," I said. "And that was Cass tired. Can you imagine what she's like on a full night's sleep?"

Wolf smiled and shook his head.

"Today the village council asked that I help you feel settled," Wolf said. "I guess you got a little lost yesterday and wandered into the pavilion during a meeting?"

"Yes," I said. "Was it . . . a problem?"

"Oh, no, of course not," Wolf said. "Everyone just wants to make sure you have the best experience possible here. We really think that you'll enjoy the art class."

"I hope so," I said. "I'm feeling kind of stuck. I'm trying to create a portrait of myself for this jour-ney. I'm not a perfectionist, but nothing about it is working."

"That's the worst," Wolf said in a way that made me think he really understood. "At least, that's what I hear. My sister is an artist, and she used to tell me that she hated when she had the desire to create but couldn't get into the flow."

"That's exactly it!" I said. It was a relief to share my experience with someone who seemed to really understand. "What kind of work does your sister do?"

"Mosaics mostly," Wolf said. "She likes to use old ceramics. Broken bowls and pieces of glass. Discarded objects, as long as they have some color. She breaks them into small pieces and then reassembles them to make something new."

"I've never worked with mosaics before!" I exclaimed. This was just what I needed! The inspiration of another's passion. And exploring another medium could give me the jump start I needed. "Would your sister mind if I looked at her work?"

Wolf paused for a moment, looked around, and then said, "Lookout Point is our destination."

"I'd really rather see one of your sister's mosaics if I could," I said. "They sound so inspiring."

"I don't know if that's a good idea. . . ."

"Really? Why not?" I asked.

"You know what, never mind," Wolf said. "Let's take a detour. We can be a few minutes late."

"Great!"

We went off the path of the arrows and through

an unmarked trail in the woods until we came upon a small shed that was hidden under the trees. Wolf removed several tree branches, unlocked the door, and took me inside the studio. The building was old and didn't look like any place else in Harmony Glen. The ceiling had beams that were laced with cobwebs. The windows were nothing more than open spaces with broken screens. The paint on the walls was peeling. I realized then just how polished and perfect everything in Harmony Glen was compared with this. And yet . . .

"This place is beautiful," I whispered. I wasn't sure why I felt I had to speak so softly except that this building seemed like a secret.

"Thanks," Wolf said. "It once belonged to my grandmother, who was also an artist. And then my mother, and then my sister."

"Where is the rest of your family?" I asked, studying the various art forms on display: sculptures, paintings, watercolors, and weavings.

"My parents died when my sister, Stella, and I were young, in the terrible storm—when Harmony Glen was almost wiped off the map."

"How awful," I said, my heart breaking for him. "I know what it's like to miss your family."

"Really?" he asked.

I nodded. "But tell me more about you. What was it like when the storm came?"

"It got pretty crazy. So many people lost their homes. There was lots of fighting. Food supplies became limited. Resources of all kinds were scarce. Neighbors were looting neighbors," Wolf said. "It was a joke that the name of our town was Harmony Glen."

"That sounds so scary," I said.

"It was. I can still remember what it felt like to scrounge for food at night with Stella, huddling under blankets to keep warm. We were so hungry and tired. That is, until Joaquin stepped up, created the village council, and built the walls, almost closing off the northern entrance completely—"

"That's how we came in. It was hard to find," I said.

"Yes. And he installed a big gate at the southern entrance. It's never locked, but it *could* be. And for some reason . . ." Wolf said, his brow furrowing, "I think that made us all feel safe again."

"I see. Where is Stella now?" I asked. "Is she taking the art class, too? I'd love to meet her."

"No, um . . . You see, Stella went dark," Wolf said. He closed his eyes, shaking his head.

"I'm not sure what that means," I said tentatively.

"She lost all of her stars, and then she ran away," he said.

"How did she lose her stars?" I asked.

"I really shouldn't be talking about this. Can we change the subject?" he asked.

"Of course," I said. "I'm sorry she's . . . gone. You must really miss her."

"We shouldn't focus on the past. As Joaquin says, only the now is real."

"I see," I said, noticing he suddenly seemed genuinely nervous. "Why don't you show me some of her work?"

Wolf revealed a mosaic of a woman with a strong face and determined eyes. His eyes shone as though he were happy to share it with someone. "It's her self-portrait. Her best work, I think."

"It's amazing!" I said, admiring the details. The piece was composed of thousands of pieces of various materials all against a white backdrop. The effect was stunning. All the parts worked together to create what felt like a living, breathing work of art. There were some greenish-blue pieces, however, that stood out among the others. They were bright, shiny, and the color was almost unearthly.

"What are these made of?" I asked, running my finger over a cluster of them that had been used to create her eyes.

"That's bog moss," Wolf said.

"What? How?"

"If it's heated at the right temperature it becomes a precious metal, as strong as iron and as beautiful as, well, this."

"Amazing. I've never heard of moss turning to metal," I mused, stepping back to admire the picture again. The intricacy of it all made me a little dizzy. "My other question is . . . how did Stella ever have the patience? This would be such intricate work."

"She always focused on one feature at a time," he replied. "She said that if she thought about the whole picture at once, she'd go crazy." He smiled. "Now, I'm afraid we'd better get to Lookout Point, or our absence will be noticed."

"Let's go," I said. But all I could think about was talking to Cass about Wolf and his sister. He had not been okay when he'd described her "going dark." Clearly, Cass was onto something about Harmony Glen not being quite as perfect as it seemed, and we needed to get to the bottom of it. "But will you please meet me back here in the afternoon?"

"I really shouldn't," Wolf said.

"Don't worry," I told him, putting my hand on his shoulder. "You're safe with me."

15

CASSANDRA

"**L**ance, are you okay?" I asked. "What's going on?"

We were at rehearsal, where my only job was moving scenery around the stage—including myself. (Because, let's be honest, I was scenery, too.) While Alfonso was having a private conference with Eugene, Lance paced the stage, looking sick with worry.

"Did you see something suspicious?" I asked. "Because now not only do I think something is weird about this place, I have proof." I was about to tell him about our discovery in the library when he started talking.

"Tree, you speaketh!" Lance said.

"Oh, no," I said, realizing that Lance had not been quietly observing as I'd hoped—he'd simply been getting into character!

"Thy voice is a pox upon my pheasants," Lance said.

"Seriously?" I asked.

"Ever since you moved the shade of your tree, I've lost two of my birds. I am a minder of the pheasants, after all. It is my duty here in Harmony Glen, but with your unreliable shade, a pheasant minder is at a great loss," Lance continued.

"Okay, that's taking it a little far," I said, taking a step backward. "There are no pheasants and I'm a person, not a tree. So."

"*La, la, la,*" Hook Foot sang as he flapped his wings.

Apparently, I was on the road trying to save the kingdom—with a theater troupe!

Just then, Raps came into the auditorium.

"Cass, can I, um, talk to you for a moment?" she asked, her voice full of urgency.

"Of course!" I said, leaping off the stage.

"Dear Princess," Alfonso said with a deep bow, "we are most glad to have you here, gracing Harmony Glen. However, we are in rehearsals, and Tree is needed for this scene."

"Really?" I asked.

"Who else is going to move the props?" he asked.

I looked at Lance, who gaped in horror.

"You'll find a way," I said, strolling up the aisle. "The princess of Corona needs me, and that's my day job. You understand, right?"

"You are so cruelly indifferent to my pheasants," Lance said.

"Because they don't exist," I said, taking Rapunzel by the arm.

"Do you need me?" Eugene asked.

"I got this, Fitzherbert," I said.

"We'll talk back at the caravan," Rapunzel said to him. When I joined her by the door, she ushered me outside.

"What's going on?" I asked.

"So I think you were onto something when you said this place gave you a bad feeling," Rapunzel said.

"Tell me what happened," I said, leading her away from the building toward a cluster of trees.

Abigail walked by and Rapunzel politely waved to her.

"I met Wolf today," Rapunzel whispered as we walked down a path that seemed private.

"He's a good guy," I said.

"And he mentioned something strange about their star charts," she continued. "His sister lost all her stars and now she's missing. He claims she ran away, but it doesn't make sense to me. They were all the family each other had."

"Where are we going?" I asked as some children passed us.

"You'll see."

Rapunzel checked over her shoulder and then guided me off the well-marked path, through a forest. Wherever we were going was off the trail. *Way* off. At last, we arrived at a ramshackle building that appeared to be at the very edge of Harmony Glen.

"This is Wolf's sister's secret art studio. I want you to hear the story from him. He doesn't want to utter a word of it outside of here."

Rapunzel knocked on the door quietly and Wolf opened it.

"So your sister is missing?" I asked.

"She ran away," Wolf said, shooting Rapunzel a look.

"Wolf," Rapunzel said. "You can trust Cass."

Wolf looked me right in the eye. I didn't blink. "I want to help," I said.

"She went dark," Wolf said with a sigh. "It was a shame. Obviously, Harmony Glen isn't for everyone."

"I promise you can be honest with us," Rapunzel

said, placing a hand on his. "I lived without my family for a long time, and I, *we*, don't want you to be without yours any longer."

He nodded, clearly upset.

"She lost her stars, right?" Rapunzel asked.

"That's right," he said. "We call that going dark. It rarely happens. In fact, it's only happened two other times."

"When?" I asked.

Wolf held his breath. Raps put her hand on my shoulder as if to tell me *One thing at a time.*

"Sorry," I said. "We didn't see them take away any stars last night. It seemed like they were just handing them out."

"Some nights are like that. And I'm sure that was because you are here. They don't want anyone to think Harmony Glen is anything less than perfect."

"Who, exactly, is 'they'?" Rapunzel asked.

"The village council," Wolf said. "Joaquin, Abigail, Martina, and Alfonso."

"But they seem so nice," Rapunzel said.

"They are," Wolf replied. "You need to understand that I shouldn't be telling you this. It's just, I really miss my sister. They said she ran away, but I don't think she'd ever leave me. Ever since we lost our parents in the great storm, she promised she would always be by my side."

"From everything that you've told me about her, I'm sure that's true," Rapunzel said, stepping into the little kitchen.

"What makes someone lose stars?" I asked.

"It's complicated," Wolf said.

"We can handle complicated," I said.

"Your story is important and we want to hear it," Rapunzel said as she emerged with a plate of cookies. Of course, it had only taken Raps a few minutes to find something sweet to make Wolf feel better.

"It happens when someone doesn't work for the good of the community," Wolf answered.

"Did Stella do something . . . bad?" I asked.

"It depends on what you think is bad," Wolf said. "Our parents always taught us to ask questions and be curious. She was asking about removing the chart and trying to get a petition signed. She claimed that the new Harmony Glen was too rigid and oppressive. She said there wasn't room for self-expression. Before the great storm, this place was a mecca for artists, even if we did have some crime."

"Her artwork is so expressive," Raps said, running her hand along the edge of one of the pieces.

"Ouch!" She pulled her hand back. She was bleeding a little.

"You okay?" I asked.

"Fine," Raps said, and nodded, but she was holding her wounded finger in the air.

"I'll get you a bandage," Wolf said, reaching into a cupboard. "Stella's rough around the edges, and so is her work!"

As Wolf handed me the cloth and I wrapped Raps's finger, I kept questioning him. "Let me get this straight: it's against the law to speak out?"

"No. There are no laws here," Wolf said, growing more animated. "The only rule is to do what is best for all. But Stella thought the chart wasn't best for all. She thought there might be a better way of doing things. She didn't get in trouble for signing the petition, though Joaquin did try to talk her out of it. Instead she lost stars for other reasons, like being late to her work assignments, or asking to be transferred to other assignments, even taking too much pie. Little things.

"But the fewer stars you have, the fewer opportunities you have to do what you wish. And the more you have to prove yourself. Stella was assigned to work in a pasture far away all by herself. And when she came into town one day because she wanted to see me, well . . . that was it. She lost her final star."

"I thought if she went anywhere it would be here. But there was no trace that she'd been back ever since."

"Wolf, do you really believe she ran away?" I asked.

"No," he said after just a brief hesitation. "I believe she was taken."

16

RAPUNZEL

"What are we going to do?" I asked Cass on our way to lunch at the Sunshine Cantina. I felt I had to whisper because we were back on one of the marked paths. Wolf had been really clear that he could lose stars if anyone found out he was speaking negatively about Harmony Glen to us.

"Exactly what I said," Cass replied. "Get out of here." I opened my mouth to speak, but Cass put up her hand. "And don't talk to me about letting people down. It's just a play—I think Joaquin can play the role of Flynn Rider just fine. Just like he has done every year."

"I was thinking about Wolf," I said. "He needs to know what happened to his sister."

"Maybe she did run away," Cass said.

"Do you think she did?" I asked.

"Anything's possible," Cass said.

"And leave behind her only relative? Why would anyone leave her family like that?"

"Because they have a greater purpose. I left my father. You, too, left your parents behind," she said.

"But I told them I was leaving, and they told me to go. And I plan to return. That's really different," I said.

"Maybe Stella thought that Wolf would be in a worse position if he knew where she was headed," Cass said.

"I guess that's possible," I said.

"Wait, follow me. I know how to fix your finger," Cass said when we reached a crossroads in the path. One sign pointed to the Sunshine Cantina and the other to the bog.

"Yay! We're going to the bog?" I asked as Cass led me down the more overgrown trail. With every step the air felt more humid.

"Yes," she said. "That weird blue moss water healed my foot."

"I can't believe I haven't seen it yet. And to think

I almost forgot about it! I mean, Eugene said if I hadn't seen a bog, I hadn't lived," I said as I picked up the pace.

"Your enthusiasm makes you so speedy," Cass said, practically jogging to keep up with me.

"Wow," I said when we got there. A swarm of bright yellow three-winged butterflies danced above us. An adorable family of ducks waddled through the swamp grass. Blue frogs, the same color as the moss, croaked back and forth from big lily pads. "This place is so . . . full of life."

"I know. But it doesn't exactly make you want to go for a dip," Cass said as her boot squelched in the mud. "It's not like the Lost Lagoon. But if you stick your hand in there, your cut will heal."

I rolled up my sleeve and sank my hand in the murky water. Immediately, my skin began to tingle in a soothing way. After a minute, I pulled my arm back and saw that my wound had closed up.

"Amazing," I said, studying my finger.

"Shhh," Cass said, pointing toward a bend in the trail. We ducked behind some bushes. Not far away, a figure dressed in camouflage clothing was taking some measurements with a rope.

"It's Joaquin," I whispered.

"I saw him here the other day, too," Cass said.

"Collecting samples. He's up to something. I say we confront him."

"No," I said, following my instincts. Cass seemed a little surprised by my definitive tone, but she didn't challenge me. Instead, we crouched in silence and watched him appear to descend below the bog.

"Um, what just happened?" I said.

"Is there a tunnel?" Cass asked.

"There has to be. Either that or a steep drop-off," I whispered back.

"This terrain is flat," Cass said. "I've surveyed it for my map."

"Maybe he's performing some kind of research . . . for medicinal purposes?" I said. "We shouldn't draw any conclusions yet. Let's watch this play out a little longer."

But Joaquin didn't reappear, and eventually, Cass and I grew tired of waiting. As soon as we were back on the path, I headed toward the Sunshine Cantina.

"Whoa, whoa," Cass said, crossing her arms. "I'm not having lunch with those weird people. Let's leave them to their science experiments. We need to pack the caravan and get going."

"Cass, I know you want to head out, but I can't leave Wolf—especially not after what we just saw," I said. "He needs our help. And we're so good when we work together. We'll be able to get to the bottom of this."

We stood at the crossroads and faced each other.

"Raps, my job is to take care of you—always. And sometimes that might mean leaving other people to fight their own battles," Cass said.

"You know me," I said, and leveled my gaze at her. "Leaving a person in trouble is not my style."

Cass sighed. "You're not budging, are you?"

I shook my head. "I know what it's like to miss my family. I know what family means. And I know that I can help."

"Okay, fine. You win. So what are we going to do?" Cass said.

I grinned. There was nothing Cass and I couldn't do together.

"You two are on your way to the Sunshine Cantina for lunch, I hope?" someone said behind us.

"Hi there," I said, turning to see Abigail. We smiled at each other. I studied her face, looking deep into her eyes. If Joaquin had some sort of plan, would she be a part of it as a member of his village council? She didn't seem sinister. And she certainly didn't seem like she could be behind separating an orphaned brother and sister. *Had Stella run away?*

"Today's special is sure to be delicious," she said. "Are you coming?"

"Yes," I said firmly.

"Oh, good," Abigail said. "And you enjoyed your morning with the painting class?"

"I took a little detour," I said. "I find this natural beauty so inspiring. I just had to experience the Great Bog!"

"We saw . . . many life-forms," Cass said, cocking an eyebrow. "Some more pleasant than others."

"It's a magical place." Abigail laughed. "And you, Cassandra, don't you have play rehearsal?"

"I'm a tree," Cass said. "I think I have it down."

A gentle breeze rustled the leaves above us. I felt my feet on the ground and stood tall. Something in me knew it was a risk, but I had to ask anyway—my heart told me that Abigail was good and kind.

"I have a question for you, Abigail. I heard about an artist today. I believe she works mostly in mosaics. Her name is Stella. Do you know her?" I asked.

A shadow crossed Abigail's face.

"Stella is indeed a talent, but I'm afraid that she ran away a little while ago," Abigail said as we continued down the path together.

"Ran away?" I asked. "Why would anyone want to run away from here?"

"It's a good question," Abigail said. "But Harmony Glen just isn't for everyone."

"Someone made a quick costume change," Cass said under her breath when Joaquin entered the Sunshine Cantina, looking as tidy and clean as could be in his usual crisp suit. We were sitting at a lovely table decked out in linen with purple flower arrangements. Joaquin even had a matching violet in his lapel. Only thirty minutes before he'd been wearing totally different clothes as he'd trudged through muck.

Cass's surveillance skills were sharp. I could learn from this; practicing being more observant would serve me well, both on this journey and as queen.

Just then, our waiter, the quiet man Abigail had said was called Edmond, placed steaming food in front of us.

"Thank you," I said, taking in the tasty-looking (and -smelling) dish: lentils and potatoes stewed in fragrant spices served atop freshly picked vegetables, with hot crusty bread and an array of chutneys for dipping.

I was determined to practice my observation

skills right there and then. What kind of person was Edmond? And why was he so quiet?

"This looks so delicious," I said. Edmond simply nodded. "Have you tried it?" He shook his head. I gazed into his eyes. There was a story there, I could feel it. And yet, he didn't want to share it. He bowed and walked away.

I leaned over to Cass and whispered: "What we need to do is get more involved in the community and really talk to people. And I think the only way we'll learn more is if we play along and really embrace the jobs we've been given."

"How am I supposed to get into my job as a tree?" Cass asked as she munched on some bread.

"Maybe you can ask for a new job?" I said.

Eugene entered and was seated at a long table. All the children of Harmony Glen gathered around him. He was telling a story—a Flynn Rider story, no doubt.

"I see someone has found his place," Cass said. Then she paused and seemed to admit against her will, "I like this chutney."

"Cassandra and Rapunzel, I hope that you had a most excellent morning," Joaquin said as he approached us.

"Yes," I said. "In fact, we are feeling like we want to be even more a part of Harmony Glen. Would it be okay if I taught a painting workshop? I was hoping to get started on that mural for the festival."

"By all means," Joaquin said. "That is absolutely the spirit of Harmony Glen. Everyone pitching in, whether they are a princess or a pauper."

"And I'd like to teach a fighting skills class," Cass said.

"We don't have any need for fighting skills here," Joaquin said. "You may have noticed that we live in remarkable peace."

Daphne handed us two glasses of lavender lemonade.

"This is so delicious," I said. "What if Cass taught . . . fitness? Just for fun."

Cass looked horrified for exactly a second before she recovered and said, "Great idea. Perfect."

"Fitness for fun! That would be wonderful, as long as it doesn't interfere with your play rehearsals, of course," Joaquin said.

"I don't think I'll be missed," Cass said. She turned to me. "What is it about this place that everyone thinks being a tree is such a big deal?"

Eugene noticed me from across the room and smiled.

"We're going to have to help the thespian connect the dots," Cass whispered.

I waved him over.

"Hi," Eugene said. His eyes were sparkling, and it was clear he was brimming with happiness.

"Can I speak with you outside?" I asked.

"Of course," Eugene said with a grin. We stepped into the sunlight outside. A sweet breeze caused the trees with purple blossoms to tremor, dropping some of their delicate leaves on the ground. "Can you believe the weather here?"

"It's perfect," I said. "Actually, everything here *seems* perfect, but—"

"The more I think about it, the more I'm sure that Alfonso is the one who defaced the library," Eugene said. "He's very threatened by my swagger."

I sighed, trying to find the right words. I knew Eugene was enamored with Harmony Glen, and I didn't like bursting his bubble. "I know you love it here, but I'm starting to get some more information," I said. "I think Cass is right to be suspicious of this place."

"Cass is right?" Eugene said. "I find that very hard to believe."

"Something strange *is* going on here," I said, taking his arm and looking him in the eye. "We all need to be on the lookout. I made a friend this morning and he told me he was worried about his sister who ran away. And there may be more to the story."

"You know I take any concern you have very seriously," Eugene said. "But just because someone ran away doesn't mean that there's something wrong."

"And Cass and I saw Joaquin at the bog, measuring things and disappearing into tunnels."

"Well, that makes total sense," Eugene said. "He loves the bog and anyway, it's endlessly fascinating! Did you know it has healing properties?"

"Yes, I do. And yet . . . I have a bad feeling," I said.

"Then we should ask Joaquin directly," Eugene said. He didn't look worried at all.

"Eugene, a sweet young man lost his sister," I said.

"That's tragic," Eugene said, his face softening. "And all the more reason why I think we should talk to Joaquin. He's a great guy and a great leader; I doubt he'd ever let anything happen to someone in Harmony Glen."

17

EUGENE

"Joaquin," I said, waving him over. "The lovely, intelligent, and brave Rapunzel has a question for you."

"Please, ask me anything!" Joaquin said, as though he'd been waiting for the opportunity.

Rapunzel looked uneasy, and for a second I wondered if I'd put her on the spot, but she stood tall, looked him in the eye, smiled, and said, "Hello, Joaquin."

How is it possible for a person to imbue only two words with such charm and grace? Leave it to my girl.

Joaquin bowed. "Please let me know how I may

be of service to you, Princess. How are you finding it here?"

"Oh, it's great," she replied. I placed an arm around her waist, proud to be her fellow. "The citizens of Harmony Glen have been so welcoming to us—all of us. Obviously, Eugene makes a perfect Flynn Rider." Joaquin nodded. "And our friends Hook Foot and Lance are so enjoying their time in the theater."

"Lance's dedication is admirable. And Hook Foot's dance solo is . . . coming along," Joaquin said.

"And if that weren't enough, Max and Fidella have never been so spoiled," Rapunzel continued.

"We take great pride in our horses," Joaquin said.

"Naturally, Cassandra will excel at teaching Fitness for Fun," Rapunzel said.

"Good. . . ." Joaquin said, his smile slackening ever so slightly.

"It's *my* impression that I'd like to tell you about," Rapunzel said, shifting ever so slightly. I held my breath—tough questions were ahead.

"Please," Joaquin replied. "Go right ahead."

"As you know, I'm an artist," Rapunzel said. The sun was descending behind her, setting off her hair in a golden halo around her. Her smile was infectious. It was clear her words were genuine and from the heart. So why was I nervous? "I heard about a fellow artist today. Stella, the sister of a young man named Wolf."

Joaquin smiled quickly and broadly.

Abigail joined us with a tray of lavender lemonades. We each took one.

"Do you know them?" Rapunzel asked, her green eyes sparkling.

"I know everyone in Harmony Glen," Joaquin said. He was still smiling, but now he was stroking his beard rapidly. "Wolf is a great shot with the bow and arrow. And his sister is a very talented artist."

"I think so, too," Rapunzel said. "Wolf has been very kind to us. And I've never worked with mosaics before, but Stella's pieces . . ." She trailed off for a heartbeat but got right back to it. "Well, I got to see some of her work and it was stunning."

I stiffened—there was an undeniable current in the air. Were Rapunzel and Cassandra right? Was something off-kilter there? I had no sooner had the thought than Joaquin placed a reassuring hand on my back and said, "Have you met Wolf, Eugene?"

"No, I've been so busy with rehearsals," I said.

"Rapunzel here is spot-on. He's a remarkable

person, a valued member of the community," Joaquin said. Lines of joy spread from his eyes to the corners of his mouth.

Joaquin did seem to be listening to Rapunzel and acknowledging her points. Wasn't that what good leaders did?

"But I was wondering, what happened to his sister?" Rapunzel asked.

"Rumor has it she went dark," Cass chimed in, seeming to appear out of nowhere.

Where had *she* come from? It was almost as though she'd been waiting for us to have this conversation with Joaquin. Either that or she'd gotten really good at her role in the play and was becoming an expert at blending into the scenery.

"What a shame that was," Joaquin said, shaking his head.

"A terrible loss," Abigail chimed in. "I really *liked* Stella."

"So did Wolf," Cass said.

"Look, Stella didn't like it here," Joaquin said. "It was unfortunate for us. What a loss of talent. She could be hard at work at our village improvements as we speak."

"How could anyone not like it here?" I asked. Everyone there seemed genuinely happy . . . well, everyone except for Cass.

Joaquin laughed deeply.

"Some say that she disappeared," Cass said, her voice like a knife through the air.

"Disappeared?" Joaquin asked. "Like a magic trick?"

"Something like that," Cass said.

"I suppose that's one way of putting it," Joaquin said. "Though I find that language . . . misleading."

"Indeed," said Abigail.

"Then where did she go?" Rapunzel asked, crossing her arms. I was really curious now.

"Haven't you ever heard the saying that the simplest answer is almost always the correct one?" Joaquin said. He dropped his smile and met Rapunzel's firm gaze. "She just didn't like it here."

"Stella left of her own free will," Abigail added. "It's a terrible misfortune, but one we must bear no matter how difficult."

"But she was, I mean *is*, an artist," Rapunzel said. "If artists are good, they must think beyond themselves. They need to discover a truth."

"I never thought of it that way before," Abigail said.

Joaquin inhaled deeply. "Stella was just unhappy—plain and simple. And unhappy people find themselves at odds in Harmony Glen. Perhaps she journeyed on to Vardaros."

"We'll be there soon," Rapunzel said.

"Maybe we'll see her," Cassandra said. "Should we send her your regards?"

"By all means!" Joaquin said, shaking his head again. "And understandably, Wolf is upset about his unfortunate sister. I hope that he doesn't lose his way. These things can run in the family."

"This would only be a 'thing' if other people had 'vanished' as well. And no one else has vanished, right?" I asked.

"It's people like you I wish would stay forever," Joaquin said, and he patted me on the arm. Then he turned toward the ice cream bar.

"Can you just clear one more thing up for us?" Cass asked Joaquin before he left.

"Absolutely," Joaquin said, turning back. He looked a little put out, but who could blame him? That ice cream did look really good. "What's on your mind?"

"I was wondering why Harmony Glen isn't on any new maps," Cass said. "Not even the atlas in the library."

"You are an inquisitive soul, aren't you, Cassandra?" Joaquin asked.

"You could say that," Cass answered.

"You seek complications, but again, the answer is simple," Joaquin said. "After the great storm, when all of our buildings were wiped away, we were nothing but a band of ragged survivors. There was no town here, so maps everywhere were amended. We have really pulled together as a community to rebuild. We wanted to come back in style, fully functioning, and as beauteous as ever. As soon as our town emblem is complete, we'll invite all the mapmakers to visit us and document our great new Harmony Glen. We simply wanted some privacy until we got back on our feet."

"That seems like a reasonable explanation," I said, trying to make sense of it all. I hadn't seen anything *that* suspicious. So their customs were a little weird. Maybe ours were, too, to visitors.

"Now, if you'll excuse me, I have some business to attend to," Joaquin said, now heading for the door.

"Of course!" I said. I almost felt sorry for him. Cass and Raps had put him through the ringer.

"You're not going to have any ice cream?" Cassandra asked.

Joaquin turned suddenly, as if taken aback, and then replied, "Not today."

"I noticed you were about to head toward the bog," Cassandra said. "Any reason?"

"Peace," Joaquin said. "Peace."

"So, unhappy people leave," Rapunzel said to

Abigail after he'd left, "because Harmony Glen just isn't the place for them?"

"That's right," she said, speaking for the first time in a while. Then she frowned. Very quickly, she leaned in and whispered, "My sweetheart left as well—without so much as a good-bye."

And without another word, she slipped away.

18
RAPUNZEL

"Abigail," I said, hurrying after her. Cass was close behind.

"She didn't have to tell us that," Cass whispered. "She wanted us to know."

We caught up with her just as she was entering the cantina's kitchen.

"Abigail, wait," I said. She turned to us and I lowered my voice. "We'd love to talk with you about this more. Somewhere private, if you'd like?"

"I can't," she answered, though her eyes seemed to suggest otherwise.

"You can trust us," Cass said.

"Please, don't ask me anymore," Abigail replied,

her usual smile replaced by a firm expression. "I shouldn't have said anything. It just slipped out."

Cass opened her mouth to respond, but I touched her arm to stop her. I knew we shouldn't push Abigail. Now we could only go back to our original plan—get to know the other villagers better.

While the town of Harmony Glen took their afternoon siesta, Cass decided to prep for her Fitness for Fun class, which was probably a good way for her to release some steam. Our conversation with Joaquin had gotten her more than a little worked up.

Feeling as though I needed a moment to clear my head as well, I found a spot to sit alone and draw. I was determined to get my picture right in the group portrait. I had been inspired by Stella's artwork, and I wanted to create something meaningful as well. I thought about the energy and life behind her work. I closed my eyes, remembering what I'd felt when I'd been in the presence of her art. Even though I had never met her, it had struck me as completely authentic. That was what I was going for. One of those perfect Harmony Glen breezes blew across my face, combing my hair as if with gentle hands. I lifted my pencil and began.

I tried not to judge my work.

I tried not to critique it.

I tried to let it flow.

But when I stepped back to take a look at it, it was still . . . off.

I stood up and stomped my feet in frustration. Here was the trouble with trying! Wasn't an artist always supposed to try her hardest? And if not, why was trying messing me up so badly? It was as if an artist had to try really hard and then not try at all, but how was I supposed to do that?

Pascal, seated on my shoulder, looked at the portrait and shook his head.

"I know, I know," I said. "I guess I should just stop for the day?"

Pascal shrugged.

The truth was that the setting sun was a relief to me. The day was closing like a book, and I could put it aside—for now.

Pascal and I went to visit Max and Fidella in their stalls. They'd never looked so good in all their lives. I petted them and fed them apples, and soon enough it was time for dinner, and then Evensing.

"I guess tonight I won't be trying out any new guitar solos," I said to Cassandra as we headed toward the village center.

"Nope," Cass said, locking arms with me. "Tonight we watch and learn."

"Did you know that this is what the villagers call the pink hour?" Eugene said, basking in the dusky light. I could tell he was trying to change the subject. "Sometimes beautiful places are just that. Beautiful." As the sun sank behind the hills, it was true that the world had a warm rosy glow to it. The golden spire of the town center appeared like the sun itself. In the distance, bells from that tower signaled the end of the day. If I strained a bit, I thought I heard the voices of the children's choir.

"If all you want to see is the pink hour, then that's what you'll see. But we are looking deeper than that," Cassandra said. "Right, Rapunzel?"

"It's true," I said.

"I appreciate that you do look deeper, Cassandra," Eugene said, smiling as he walked down the path.

"But . . . ?" Cassandra said, vocalizing what I was thinking. Eugene and Cassandra rarely complimented each other. I could probably count on my fingers the times that they had.

"No buts," Eugene said. "I just appreciate it. I appreciate you, including your . . . foibles. Oh, look, Hook Foot and Lance are up ahead! You know, I've never seen Lance so dedicated to anything in his life, and Hook Foot has real talent. It must run in the family. I'm going to go see them so we can run lines for a few minutes. An actor's work is never done."

Cass and I watched him practically skip up the path to meet Hook Foot and Lance. The three of them really did seem as happy as could be. The place was having a positive influence on them.

"Do you realize that Eugene just said that he appreciated me and my 'foibles'?" Cass said.

I nodded. "I didn't see that coming, either."

"First of all, what kind of a word is 'foibles'?" she asked. I shrugged. Pascal giggled. "And second of all, he *appreciates* me? I don't think so."

"I think we have to take him at his word," I said. There hadn't been a trace of sarcasm in his voice.

"Well, I think it's the best proof we have that something is definitely up with this place," Cass said.

Immediately, I spotted Abigail. Cass nodded and I approached her.

"Abigail," I said, rushing to greet her. "I'm so happy to see you!"

I opened my arms to hug her, but she demurely curtsied.

"And you as well, Princess," she said, but she wouldn't meet my gaze. "Please excuse me," she said, and before I could say another word, she had disappeared into the crowd. I told myself it was because the bells were chiming the signal for the Evensing dance.

"Wolf!" Cass called, waving to our friend.

I waved, too. I was eager to catch up with him. I wanted to tell him that Cass and I were on a mission now. We were going to help him find his sister. We were going to get to the bottom of whatever was going on there. But he didn't wave back; instead, his face paled.

"Come on," I said to Cass, signaling for her to follow me as I made my way to Wolf.

"Are you okay?" I asked.

"I'm fine as can be," Wolf said.

"Because before, when you told us your story, I felt such sadness," I began.

"Only the now is real," he said, reciting the familiar Harmony Glen line. He smiled, but his eyes didn't.

"Can we just all admit that makes no sense?" Cass said.

"Look," Wolf said. "I shouldn't have said anything to you. I was out of line. I was simply caught up in the discussion of art. I didn't mean it."

"Didn't mean it?" I asked. Stella's artwork was still in my mind. How could Wolf change his mind so quickly? He studied the ground, pursed his lips, and inhaled sharply. "We want to help you," I continued.

"And your sister," Cass added. "We know something isn't right."

"If you want to help me, then please, leave me alone," Wolf said.

"How can we when—" Cass began.

But as the music swelled and the same dance that had kicked off the ceremony the night before began again, I squeezed Cass's elbow in warning. We were making things harder for him, not easier.

"Would you care to dance?" Abigail asked Wolf, inviting him to join the rest of the community.

"Absolutely," Wolf said with a smile. They bowed to each other and waved their white handkerchiefs, the traditional beginning invitation to the dance.

"Cass," I said, "tonight, let's try to actually learn the dance."

She nodded, though her brow was furrowed.

"If you stand back at a distance, I think you'll catch on pretty quickly," Wolf said.

"Then that's just what we'll do," I said.

"Yes," Abigail said. "That's what Eugene has done, and he's in perfect harmony with everyone else here."

I know, I thought. *And that's part of the problem.*

19

CASSANDRA

"So here's the deal. When someone breaks the rules, even a little bit, they lose stars," I said to Rapunzel as we both guzzled water from our goblets. We were fit, but those dances were no joke. One had to be in good shape to keep up. Maybe that was Joaquin's way of keeping anyone from ever having a meaningful conversation.

Raps and I had done everything we could to fit in that night. That was our strategy. A soldier's first objective is always to understand her surroundings. Without that, she'd be disoriented. That was another reason my father had encouraged me to study cartography. "Know the area. Know the people. You can't defend yourself against what you don't know," he'd said.

Raps downed her goblet of water and then turned to me, nodding.

"Let's see what happens now."

The chart unfurled from the high tower. My eyes zeroed in on Wolf's name, and I almost gasped. He'd lost two stars. He was down to one! No one else had just one. No wonder he had been panicking earlier. It seemed our talking to him had brought him down.

I tried to make eye contact with him, but he was looking away, wearing a brave face.

"I'd like to draw attention to a particular shift," Joaquin said.

Raps and I exchanged glances. Could this be about Wolf?

"If you've noticed, I've moved Eugene Fitzherbert to the honorary citizens' portion of the board," Joaquin said. "The village council and I agree that his dedication to the community, to the play, and to the spirit of Harmony Glen warranted this decision."

I did my best not to roll my eyes, but I guess my best wasn't good enough, because my eyes seemed to roll on their own.

"You all know how much I adore playing the role

of Flynn Rider, but as Harmony Glen prepares for a better future, I need to dedicate myself to the greater tasks at hand," Joaquin went on.

I elbowed Rapunzel. What was he referring to? Joaquin stepped in front of Eugene and said, "Thankfully, Eugene is here to keep our spirits up and remind us what Harmony Glen is all about: adventure, good citizenship, and community."

The crowd applauded and Eugene took a bow.

"And may I remind you," Joaquin continued, "that if you find yourself low on stars, there is no need to fear. You must simply recommit yourself to the community and the greater good."

I studied Wolf's face. He nodded. But it didn't escape me when he looked over his shoulder at us.

He still needs us, I thought. *He just can't say it.*

"I'm going to be the best Fitness for Fun instructor this glen has ever seen," I said to Rapunzel.

"And I'll be a good art teacher," she said.

"You know, we should attend each other's classes, so while one of us is leading, the other is gathering intelligence."

"Good idea."

"It's what you always say, right? We need to work together. We'll commit to the community," I said, unable to hide the sarcasm in my voice. "Like your boyfriend has."

"I'm going to talk to him," Rapunzel said, watching her beau. "I know that Eugene believes he's helping everyone here."

"Why can't he just get on board with the mission?" I asked, my voice full of frustration.

"Because he's not ready," Rapunzel said. "And anyway, I think he is doing a good thing for his part. Flynn Rider is good. See, Eugene is bringing out the best in people."

We faced the direction of Eugene, who was telling tales of bravery to a bunch of young kids.

"Let's let him work his magic while we work ours," Raps said.

"Okay," I said, trying to get us back on track. "So clearly the town has bought into this idea that their worth can be measured in stars. My question is—where have these runaways gone?"

"And are there only two?" Rapunzel asked.

As if he could read my mind, Wolf's eyes scanned the horizon.

On our way back to the caravan, Eugene announced, "I don't know if it's the fresh air, or the dancing, or just how nice everyone is here, but this place really is everything I thought it would be."

I couldn't stand it. "Eugene, you're so oblivious, even after seeing the missing manuscripts in the library. You still think everyone here is nice?"

"Hey, lighten up, Calamity Cass," Eugene said. "Just because you—"

"Whoa!" Rapunzel said. "I call a time-out!"

"Are you on your own journey?" Eugene continued, clearly shifting course. "Because that's fine. It doesn't mean you have to insult me. I am on mine, which just happens to be totally great, filled with people who appreciate me. Ah! Look at those giant yellow roses. Pardon me while I take a sniff."

"Cass," Rapunzel whispered. "Attacking him isn't the way. Give him some space. Give him some time. He may understand something we don't that will help us later on. He has his own way of doing things."

She gazed at him adoringly. It took warrior strength not to roll my eyes again.

"You really should take a sniff, Cassandra," Eugene said. "You're missing out."

Rapunzel nudged me, and so I obliged him for her sake.

I wish I could say otherwise, but it didn't smell half bad.

20

RAPUNZEL

"**A**re we all ready to have some fun with fitness?" I said to the folks who had turned up for Cass's class. She was busy making sure that the guard-training obstacle course was set up.

"Yes!" they cheered.

It was a pretty big group that had shown up, and Cass's training course looked really difficult. Actually, it all seemed intimidating—even the prizes, which looked to be a pile of weapons—so I was doing my best to make sure people didn't drop out because they were scared.

"Cass, are you sure this isn't too hard?" I asked as she hung a rope over a tree branch.

"It might be, but that's part of my technique," Cass said. "I think if I wear them down they might come forward with more information. Getting them to break down physically will loosen their tongues."

"Um . . ." I turned around to see the group of sweet townsfolk, some of whom were on the older side, and some who were pretty young, like Daphne and her sister Molly. "Break down physically?" I asked Cass. She nodded, inching the rope just a little bit higher. "Do you think that's necessary? This is supposed to be Fitness for *Fun*."

"Start stretching, people!" Cass called out, and then she leaned in and whispered. "You know what's not fun? Having family members disappear or run away. Whatever short-term pain they experience here—"

"Pain?" I said, crossing my arms and shaking my head. "No way."

"Oh, come on. You know what I mean. It's just exercise pain, which isn't real pain." She grinned.

I smiled and waved at the townspeople, who were dutifully stretching. "We're about to start!" I said. "Get ready for some fun! And remember, you don't have to complete the course if it's too hard."

"Ugh, you're a softy, Raps," Cass teased. Her expression suddenly changed from jocular to serious. "Well, well, well. Look who's decided to join us."

I turned to see Joaquin, outfitted in sportswear, jogging toward us.

"I'm going to make it extra hard now," Cass said out of the corner of her mouth.

"Hello," I called, nudging Cass with my elbow. I muttered under my breath, "Look cheerful. Don't blow our cover."

"Greetings, everyone!" Joaquin said.

"Greetings, Joaquin," the townspeople said. They seemed jittery with excitement.

"What a treat to have the princess and her maid—"

"Lady-in-waiting!" Cass said with a forced smile.

"Yes, whatever," Joaquin said. "What a treat that they are here, teaching us Coronan fun and games. Now, remember. No one can win."

"Uh . . . excuse me?" Cass said. "Why not?"

"Cassandra put a lot of effort into the prizes," I whispered to Joaquin. "They're weapons from her personal collection."

"Weapons! Oh, dear! How kind but misguided. You see, there's no winning here in Harmony Glen," Joaquin said. "If there are winners, that means there are losers. Here, we like to keep everything even. Maintains the harmony."

Cass began to speak, but I stepped on her foot, warning her.

"We understand," I said. "No winners, no losers."

"Your royal blood is evident at every turn," Joaquin said to me. "In your manners, your demeanor, your—*ahem*—diplomacy."

"Well, we're a team," I said, slinging an arm around Cassandra and clamping her arms to her body. Part of me just wanted to keep her from slugging Joaquin. "Cassandra here taught me everything I know."

I also wanted to send the message to Joaquin that I was as loyal as they come, and I would not stand for any insulting of my lady-in-waiting. In the nicest possible way, of course.

"This is just fitness for fun, not for competition," I reiterated.

"What's the point?" Cassandra asked. "I thought this was sports."

"Fun!" I said with a grin. "Fun is the point!"

"See, now that's more like it," Joaquin said. "Raising everyone's spirits and making sure they get some exercise while they're at it. It's the essence of sport. I'll go ahead and lead them in some stretches. We have a morning series they all love."

"Sounds like a great idea," I said, squeezing

Cass's hand to warn her not to say anything too confrontational.

"Doesn't Joaquin realize that he creates winners and losers every night with his stars?" Cass asked, her face red with frustration as she lowered the climbing ropes to the height I'd suggested.

"But that's just it," I said. "*He's* creating them."

"True. That way he decides who wins and who loses everything. It has nothing to do with people's talents or skills—just their ability to fit in and not make waves," Cass said as her eyes narrowed. "He and the council are in complete control."

"We have to get *them* to see that," I said, nodding at our group.

We turned to face the crowd. They were following his moves with an amazing synchronicity.

"I'll point it out right now, as clear as day!" Cass said. "What's he going to do? Kidnap me? I dare him."

"Are you two going to join us?" Joaquin asked.

"Yes, join us," a few of the citizens said.

"One second!" I called. "Cass, you need to calm down," I said softly. "We have to approach this with care. Remember that the people of Harmony Glen have been living like this for a long time. You can't just change their minds with a speech."

We walked toward the group and stood in the back, following along. I reached up and stretched to the side. Joaquin began to lead everyone in a song. It was a call-and-response with a sweet melody. It reminded me of a children's tune.

"We can't just tell them," I whispered to Cass. "We need to somehow *show* them that life can be different—that it's nice to have a hodgepodge of customs and opinions."

"Raps, revolution might be exactly what these people need," Cass said.

"A revolution from within," I said. "If we're not careful, someone might get hurt."

Cass stretched with the rest of the group, but I could see her simmering under the surface. I wasn't sure how much longer I'd be able to contain her temper.

I needed to make a decision before things got out of control.

"I think you should go to play rehearsal," I told her. "I can help lead the rest of the class and watch Joaquin."

"Why?" she asked.

"Because you're too wound up. You're about to burst," I said. "A soldier needs a level head."

She looked annoyed, but she said, "Fine. Maybe you're right."

"You go see if you can learn anything at the theater," I said. "I'll do a brief, cheerful fitness routine and then transition into art class. Come back when you feel better."

21

EUGENE

"Is it just me, or does this scene feel stale?" I said, breaking character and pacing the stage. The more I'd rehearsed, the deeper I wanted to go into the script. "This scene just doesn't have the kind of adventure that I think people will be looking for at the Flynn Rider Festival."

"Are you serious?" Cass muttered under her breath. "We're stopping again? Can't we just get through this?"

"No, Cassandra," I said.

I watched as she took a series of deep, calming breaths, the very same kind I'd seen Rapunzel take when she was coping with a situation that made her mad. Was it possible that Cass was finally picking up from Rapunzel how to be a positive influence on the world?

"Um, excuse me, Sir Rider," Lance said with a deep bow—he absolutely refused to break character. "Though I be but a townsperson, and a lowly, though diligent, pheasant watcher at that—"

"The most vigilant I could hope for," I said. Lance's dedication was nothing short of inspiring.

He nodded humbly and continued. "I feel the need to point out that your line is literally: 'Adventure awaits if we swing across this bog.' And then the stage direction reads: 'Flynn Rider brandishes his lasso and whips it in the air, where a stagehand above catches it and affixes it to a beam, and Flynn leaps over the audience.'"

"That pretty much screams adventure," Hook Foot chimed in with his normal voice. I had to bite back a laugh. With his falsetto and decent arabesques, Hook Foot was convincing as a three-winged butterfly—but when he spoke in his regular baritone, the sight of him in his gigantic wings was just funny.

"You make a good point, but it doesn't quite feel earned, does it?" I said, stroking my goatee.

"Of course it doesn't!" Cass burst out. "Because nothing here is truly earned!"

"I resent that," Hook Foot said.

"I'm getting out of here. I don't want to be a tree anymore," Cass said.

"There are no small parts," I reminded her. "Only small actors."

"Give me a break," Cassandra said.

"Cassandra, dear," Alfonso said. "Perhaps you've had too much sun? You look a bit flushed. Why don't you have some lavender lemonade and lie down?"

"I don't want to relax," Cass said. "I don't want to lie down!"

"How about some more deep breaths?" I offered. Cass could be scary, but this was extra-scary Cass.

"Look," Cass said, ripping the tree costume from her body. "This play has no life in it because there's no conflict, and there's no conflict because the people here have forgotten what conflict is, and no one wants to remind them," Cass said. "Conflict is how characters learn and grow and think and change."

"Gee, I never thought of it like that," Lance said, taking notes. "No wonder I've been stuck with Thomas."

"And it's how people grow, too—unless they aren't allowed to have conflict," Cass said.

"There's nothing worse than a bitter actress," Hook Foot said, shaking his head.

"Cassandra," Alfonso called, "if you'd like to be a townsperson, I'm sure that could be arranged. We could find someone else to play the tree."

"Like an actual tree!" Cass said. "How about that? And actually, Hook Foot, there is something worse than a bitter actress. A brainless follower, which is what every person in Harmony Glen has become. No one here wants conflict, because that would mean that someone other than the village council might be able to get ahead. You all are a bunch of followers. And if you don't wake up and see the truth soon, you're going to realize you've spent your whole lives in the same place!"

"I must admit," Alfonso said, "I'm offended and alarmed."

I looked at the faces around me. They were filled with confusion and fear. Cass could be a wet blanket, but now she was a flaming torch. And she was taking down the whole cast. "Cassandra, this is a little dramatic, don't you think?"

"It *is* dramatic. But that's what this town needs," she said.

"Excuse us," I said to the cast. I took Cassandra by the arm and led her to a quiet corner.

"I think if you are so miserable here in Harmony Glen, then maybe you should move on," I said. "We'll meet you in Vardaros after the festival."

"And leave the princess alone here?" Cassandra asked.

"She's not alone," I said. "She has me."

"Excuse me, what I *meant* to say was—leave her with no one looking out for her?"

"That was low," I said. It was an insult to the core and she knew it. "Dungeon low. And you know it's not true. I'd never let anything happen to her."

"You've drunk too much lavender lemonade if you still think that this place is safe," Cassandra said. "I have to get out of here. I've never liked it here."

"I know being out on the road is tough," I said. "Maybe a few days on your own would help clear your head?"

"*My* head isn't the one that needs clearing," Cass said. "It's time to move on." And she left.

"I'll try to talk some sense into her," Lance said, chasing after her.

Alfonso and the rest of the cast looked at me as though I might have an answer for them. Cassandra had flung a million questions into the air like a handful of confetti. What exactly had happened in the fitness class with Rapunzel that morning? Cass didn't like not getting her way, but this was off the wall.

"Well, this is awkward," I said. "Where were we?"

"You thought the scene felt stale," Hook Foot said. "And that the room lacked energy."

"Maybe we should just keep it as it is," I said.

"Hear hear," said Alfonso. "I agree."

22

RAPUNZEL

"**T**hat was fun, right?" I said, after making up a heart-racing aerobics routine and cheering everyone on in my peppiest voice.

"I loved it!" Daphne said.

"It was splendid!" Joaquin added. "Brava, Rapunzel."

"Art is a kind of fitness, too. A fitness of the mind and heart," I said to the group. "And we are going to be working on self-portraits for a great mural along the wall. Brief water break, then we'll get started!" I said.

I checked to see if Cass was coming down the path, but she was nowhere in sight. Joaquin approached me as the class drank from their canteens.

"Here is my vision for your art class," he said, gesturing broadly. "Everyone will paint their portrait from the shoulders up, facing front, with a large Flynn Rider–esque smile, just like he has on the cover of *The Tales of Flynnigan Rider*."

"Um, okay," I said, not expecting such detailed instructions.

"And the backgrounds should be bright blue sky, just like we have today," Joaquin said as he gazed upward. "Not a cloud in sight."

"Got it," I said.

"They should be painted directly on the wall. My hope is that for many years to come, our citizens will be able to regard the mural and remember that life is good here in Harmony Glen," Joaquin said.

The group gathered around. Joaquin turned to them and said, "You will all paint yourselves in the style of Flynn Rider! Noble work for the greater good! Remember, good art brings peace and order, and calms the soul."

"Not always," I said, thinking about Stella's mosaic. It had done the opposite of calm me down. It had awakened me and spurred me to action!

Joaquin breezed past my comment. "Once these portraits are painted in the cheerful hues of Harmony Glen, we'll be able to display them on the great wall as proof of the happiness of our citizens," he said. Then he clapped his hands. "Now, everyone, I must return to the leadership pavilion to attend to exciting new business for Harmony Glen. I trust that with the princess leading this class, you will find harmony in your hearts."

The class bid him good-bye and he walked up the hill. When he was out of sight, the little girl Daphne said, "We'd like to see your artwork, Rapunzel."

"Yes, we hear you're a great artist," Molly said.

"Here's what I'm working on right now," I said, showing them the picture of our group as we set out on our journey. I had painted it just a short while ago, and yet we already seemed different somehow. Hook Foot and Lance, grimacing to show their toughness in the portrait, were now in a state of theatrical bliss. Cassandra looked the same but more agitated. Eugene, who had been bothered that no one was taking him up on his road trip advice, didn't have the same glow that he had developed in Harmony Glen. Now he beamed like a lighthouse from his celebrated role. And I still looked *off* . . . too smiley, and yet not truly happy. I seemed brave, but also unsure. I looked stiff. I just wasn't myself.

"It's beautiful," Molly said.

"That's very kind, but a self-portrait is supposed to be, well, you. And to me, this doesn't quite feel like . . . like *me*."

Later, as the class worked hard on their portraits, each featuring the same blue sky, the same pose, I kept thinking that there was so much more we could do. The uniformity of the pictures left me feeling down. I wandered over to Wolf's portrait.

I know you can do better than this, Wolf, I thought.

The bells chimed, signaling that it was time to gather for Evensing.

"Okay, everybody, let's put away your supplies and we'll finish tomorrow," I said.

Though my day had been less productive than I'd hoped, I was eager to find Cass and ask if she'd learned anything else at her play rehearsal that might help us figure out just what was going on in Harmony Glen.

The sky was turning that lovely shade of pink, casting a rosy glow over the hills and on everyone's faces. Pascal hopped on my shoulder, and that's when I saw Abigail coming toward me.

"Abigail, are you okay?" I asked.

"Yes, but your friend has had a bit of a rough afternoon, I'm afraid," Abigail said.

"Cassandra?" I asked.

"I heard she stormed out of play rehearsal after some, well, *disturbing* words," Abigail said. "I have to run. Mustn't be late for Evensing."

Pascal and I looked for Cass at the caravan. She

wasn't there. I popped my head into the Sunshine Cantina, but she wasn't there, either.

Then I searched Stella's studio. I was going to be late for Evensing, but I didn't care. I needed to find Cass. When the bells rang to signal the first song, I ran to the town wall, hoping I'd find her in the crowd, but I didn't.

"I can't find Cass!" I said, my voice shaking, as soon as I saw Eugene, Lance, and Hook Foot gathering for Evensing.

"She went to Vardaros early," Eugene said. "Don't worry."

"That can't be true," I said, shaking my head. "There's no way she would have left me."

"Rapunzel, she said herself that she had to leave. She never liked it here," Eugene said.

The bells rang behind me, and their cheerfulness only added to my panic.

"Indeed," Lance said. "The words Flynn Rider spoke are but as true as gold. I heard the maid speaketh herself of her distaste for this land. And then she ran away."

"Speaketh?" Eugene said. "That's not a word."

"Well, it sounds good," Lance said.

The musicians summoned the citizens to take their positions for the dance.

"Lance," I said. He didn't respond. "Townsperson Number Four!"

"Yes," Lance said with a grin. "At your service, m'lady."

"What exactly did Cassandra say? And where did you see her running to?" I asked.

"She said that she knew something was wrong with this place and that it was time to move on."

"Like I said," Eugene chimed in.

"And then, as I was minding my pheasants—"

"Which are made out of paper and tape," Hook Foot added.

"I saw her run toward the wall at the border, beyond the hedges of color so green," Lance said, feeding directly into Hook Foot's singing a few bars of his solo for "Land So Green and Verdant."

Confusion washed over my face.

Eugene touched my arm. "I told you, Blondie. She's gone."

"She'd never leave me," I said.

"Of course not," Eugene said. "She wouldn't leave you *permanently*. But this is just for a few days. You know Cass; she's never been able to get along with others, and that's what Harmony Glen is all about!"

I took a deep breath. I needed to relax so I could actually think. Getting worked up was not going to solve anything. I needed to work extra hard to maintain a calm, rational mind.

As the music soared and Eugene, Hook Foot, and Lance all merrily danced the steps we now knew by heart, I took more deep breaths to ease my anger. How could Eugene be eating all this up without even pausing to think about it? I knew he and Cass didn't get along, but this place had really gone to his head if he honestly believed Cass would leave without telling me.

Had she been mad at me when I'd asked her to leave the exercise class that morning? Cass could really hold a grudge. Her relationship with Eugene was proof of that. Was it possible that she had just stormed off toward Vardaros, resuming the road trip like she had wanted to before? One thing was certain: I wasn't going to be able to figure any of it out if I couldn't pull myself together.

I glanced up at the dancers in front of me, noticing Abigail watching me intently.

I decided I needed to join in—now more convincingly than ever.

So I put on my best smile, and when the dance changed, I stepped in line.

"Mind if I join?" I asked, stepping between two of the girls from my art class. Wolf was directly across from me, so he would be my first partner.

"Of course not, Princess," they said.

"Greetings," Wolf said.

"Did you hear that Cass decided to leave early?" I asked.

"It's a shame she wasn't enjoying herself," Wolf said.

The dance was so fast-paced it was hard to keep up the conversation.

"She was last seen heading toward the studio," I said.

Panic flickered across Wolf's face, the tempo picked up, and it was time to change partners.

"Go back to the library," he whispered as we let go of each other's hands.

"Why?" I asked.

Ramona, he mouthed, before he turned to face his new partner.

As I danced down the line, I wondered what on earth he had meant.

PART THREE
THREE
THE RUNAWAYS RETURN

23

CASSANDRA

I awoke with a mouthful of dirt somewhere far away from Harmony Glen. I could tell because the soil was a totally different texture and, er, taste. Using my shoulder, I wiggled a blindfold off my eyes and saw that the trees were of a different variety. There were no three-winged butterflies or gigantic lilac trees. I was far from the influence of the blue moss, though I could hear sounds of rushing water nearby—a waterfall, I thought. I needed to find it. I was thirsty and had a terrible headache. It was dark and there was dew on the ground, so I knew it was probably close to dawn.

I sat up. It seemed the ropes holding my arms were loose. I shook them off and wiped my mouth, picking some leaves from my hair as I gazed up at the sky. The first thing I noticed was Owl, who was perched directly above me, keeping watch. I nodded at him and he hooted back. So he had tracked me—what a brave and trusty warrior. It could have been a perilous flight. He swooped down and landed on a low branch close by.

I was glad to have him with me, but that also meant he wasn't with Rapunzel, and I wondered if she was safe. The only comfort I had was that when she put her mind to it, she could control her temper better than I could. I was there because of my outburst at the theater.

And, of course, she had a much higher tolerance for all that "only the now is real" malarkey that the people of Harmony Glen were so into, and which Eugene (oh, the thought of him getting us into this mess made my blood boil!) had embraced like a dingbat.

Rapunzel had warned me to keep a lid on it, to make sure I just played along so we could operate smoothly, and I had lost it. Why? How had I let myself lose control like that? Was I losing my warrior instinct?

I'd been off my game ever since I'd left Corona. Usually I could read situations better than anyone else and figure out the best way to tackle a situation both physically and mentally, but the past few days I'd been the worst version of myself. I'd been trying to control everything, when, in fact, I'd just been making things worse. I'd let Eugene get under my skin too much, and then I'd been unable to manage my temper, acting before waiting for the enemy to act first. I prided myself on being able to put my opponents on their heels and then force them to lose their balance, but it was I who had lost my balance. This was all wrong.

Last night had been particularly rough. I played the scene back in my mind.

I'd gone to Stella's studio both to get away from everyone and to search for more clues. I'd thought maybe if I studied her art, I could find some hidden message about what had happened to Stella and why she had disappeared.

I hadn't even known someone else was in the room. I didn't hear a sound until it was too late. I felt their presence behind me, but before I could turn around—bam! A blindfold covered my eyes and a rope tied my hands behind my back. I struggled, kicking and flailing as much as I could. But my opponent had caught me by surprise; they had the upper hand and they knew it. I was led out of the studio and walked for hours, trying everything I could to escape and shouting at the top of my lungs. After a while, I was forced onto a boat of some kind—I could tell by the sound of lapping water and the unsteady feel of the wood beneath my boots. I must have fallen asleep, because the next thing I knew, I was there. Wherever *there* was.

I stood up and noticed that, luckily, my attacker hadn't injured me in any way.

My senses were on high alert now, however. I heard the crunch of leaves and jumped to attention.

"Be warned," I said. "I'm a Coronan warrior."

I still had my knife in my boot.

"I'm not here to hurt you," a soft voice said. A young woman stepped into the shimmering moonlight. "I'm here to see if you're okay." She extended a shaky hand. "My name is Stella."

24

RAPUNZEL

I wiped the sweat from the back of my neck and tore off yet another sheet of paper from my sketch pad. It was almost dawn and I'd been up most of the night searching for Cass. Everyone knew that Harmony Glen was free of bandits, thieves, and ruffians, but it was still unnerving to search the village through the night. If someone had the skill to kidnap Cass, they would likely be able to get me as well. And yet, I doubted a wandering band of robbers would have stopped me.

After Evensing I had headed for the library, looking for Cass and scanning the books for the name Ramona. Was she an author? A character? Was it a first name or a last? I found nothing. And then

I began to worry that the light of my torch would draw attention. I decided to go back the next day.

I refocused my efforts on searching for Cass throughout the rest of the village. From the bog to the archery field, the leadership pavilion to Wolf's studio, the town center to the entrance gate, I looked everywhere. There was no trace of her. Though what was I expecting: a trail of bread crumbs, or maybe weapons?

Finally, when the sky was at its darkest, I realized that I needed to regroup. I was exhausted. *I need sleep*, I thought. *I need to stay strong.* As I walked barefoot back to our camp, I wondered if perhaps Cass was in the most obvious place of all: our caravan. Maybe, I thought, she was also a bit thrown off by being on the road. Maybe she had struck out on her own for a while but was now simply asleep in her bunk, waiting for the moment that we left this place—a place she'd never liked or wanted to visit. I picked up the pace, running down the well-marked path. After all, weren't the answers to the most difficult questions often right in front of our eyes? I had so convinced myself this was the reality that I ran into our caravan totally expecting to see her. But only Pascal awaited me, with deep circles under his eyes. I guess he was worried, too. Cass was gone, and we both knew she hadn't left on her own. It just wasn't her.

"We'll figure this out tomorrow," I said to Pascal. And then it dawned on me that it already *was* tomorrow. "After a few hours' sleep, we'll come up with a plan." He nodded again, but we were clearly both discouraged.

But, of course, I couldn't fall asleep. Not with my best friend missing! I tossed and turned for an hour until I finally surrendered.

With an equally worried Pascal on my shoulder, I built a fire and began to sketch. Art has always been the thing that can calm me down and bring me back to my center. I couldn't control where Cass was, but I could focus on my work. Maybe, with a clear, calm center, I could strategize.

I took several deep breaths, and that's when it came to me. The image of the mosaic in Wolf's studio. It had been powerful to behold, and Wolf's words seemed to echo in my mind: *Stella focused on one detail at a time.* Maybe that was what I should do now.

The temperature in Harmony Glen really was lovely, even before dawn. It was just cold enough to want to be close to the fire, but warm enough that I didn't need a blanket around me, leaving my arms free to draw and my feet comfortable just as they were—bare. I wriggled my toes in the soft dirt.

My feet. They were strong, comfortable, capable, and free. They were best not contained. I should draw only them, I thought. Focus on one thing. And so I did. I planted my foot in the sweet earth and drew it. I felt a smile spread across my face as I sketched my toes and the hem of my dress.

It was me! I'd found myself in my feet! From there I worked upward—to my dress, my face, and, of course, my hair. My face looked like me. I'd captured my spirit with the honesty that had eluded me. I had my artistic groove back! I flipped through the pages of my notebook to the group portrait, where I looked so stiff and unlike myself. Finally, I could fix that.

Now I just had to figure out a way to fix everything else.

25

CASSANDRA

"Stella," I said, tucking my knife back in my boot and bowing my head. She appeared both very brave and scared all at once, and my warrior instinct told me that I needed to put her at ease.

Stella relaxed, placing the basket she carried on one hip. I could see the remnants of Harmony Glen's cornflower blue uniform in her clothes. It looked like she had kept the bodice, but shortened the sleeves (using the remaining fabric to tie back her hair) and made pantaloons out of the skirt.

"I'm Cassandra, from the kingdom of Corona, and I know your brother."

"Wolf! How is he?" she asked, her eyes lighting up.

"He's fine," I said, though when I remembered the last time I had seen him I couldn't help thinking of the circles under his eyes. "Though, honestly, he seems distressed. He's worried about you."

"Of course he is," she said, hanging her head. "Ever since he was born, we've never been apart. After the . . . after I was taken, I wasn't sure he'd be okay. How did you find Harmony Glen?" she asked. The sun was rising behind me and she squinted against the light.

"I actually didn't really want to visit," I said. "It is not my thing." Something about the way I said that made her laugh. I smiled in return. "I'm Princess Rapunzel's lady-in-waiting, and her boyfriend, Eugene, is a huge Flynn Rider fan. So even though we are on a very serious mission, he just had to take a detour."

"Was it what he expected?" Stella asked. There was no trace of laughter on her face now.

"It was everything he expected and more," I said. "Joaquin made him the star of the play for the Flynn Rider Festival."

"Of course he did," she muttered.

"Why would you say that?" I asked.

"No reason," she said.

Though what she really meant was *No reason*

that I'm going to tell you. How could I get her to trust me? Honesty, I realized. She had a nose for it.

"I didn't like it," I said. "It was too perfect. I thought there was something weird going on, and so I announced it. Now I find myself on this river-bank with no memory of how I got here." Stella's eyes went wide. "Sound familiar?"

And then something did come back to me. Right before I'd been struck on the head, I'd been study-ing Stella's mosaic, contemplating the blue moss. I felt around in my pocket and found a bright blue metallic piece I'd taken off the mosaic. I handed it to her.

She stared at it for a long moment. Then she shook her head.

"Come with me," she said, nodding her head toward the thick woods ahead.

"Why is Joaquin doing this?" I asked.

"He has a plan, and whoever speaks out against him or has a different opinion than him is taken by his accomplice," Stella said.

"The person who brought us here," I said.

She nodded and then stopped to pick some herbs for her basket. "And we know that it's not Joaquin who takes us, because I got a quick glance at him before he blindfolded me. He wore a mask, but he wasn't as tall and didn't have a beard. So Joaquin's not the only one involved. Now come and meet the others," she said.

I followed her toward the sound of rushing water. The sun rose on two other people, who also looked like they had been living outdoors for a while. Their camp was in view of the waterfall, which roared in the not-too-far distance. They were gathered in a circle preparing an early morning meal.

"I'm Cassandra," I said. "I'm from Corona, and I'm here to help."

"Welcome," said a man as he handed me a steaming cup of tea and a bowl of warm grains. "I'm Gray."

"And I'm Ramona," a young woman said. "Come have some breakfast."

"Tell me, how did you find one another?" I asked. "Does the masked person always drop people in the same place?"

"He leaves us close enough to find one another. We've often wondered why," Ramona said.

"We think it's someone who doesn't want to leave us all alone," Stella said. "But still wants to punish us."

"Hmmm . . ." I considered this. "What did you all do to get here?"

"I gave a speech at Evensing," Ramona said.

"About how the dances were making us all dizzy, and we'd stopped thinking for ourselves."

"But it wasn't just that that got you banished," Stella said.

"True. The Author was my great-grandfather," Ramona explained. "And I protested the way Joaquin 'edited' our library."

I remembered the missing pages in the books we'd perused, how the town had been erased from the maps there.

"There's more," Gray added.

"When the great storm was approaching, my father buried the original Flynn Rider manuscripts in a secret underground location," Ramona explained. "I'm the only one who knows where they are, and Joaquin doesn't want them to resurface. Otherwise, my great-grandfather's true message of freedom, equality, and tolerance might get out."

"Exactly. I was on the village council," Gray chimed in. "With my fiancée, Abigail."

"Of course!" I said. "Abigail spoke of you. She seems to miss you a lot."

"We suggested that the village council change every few years, but Joaquin didn't want that idea to get out."

"What did you do?" I asked.

"I went to visit Joaquin one evening to talk more about it privately, and discovered him working on some secret plans. They had to do with the bog. I don't know what they were, but as soon as he saw me looking over his shoulder, I was taken," he said.

"Does anyone else know about the secret plans?" I asked.

"Only us," Ramona said. "I believe that he wants to sell the blue moss. It's rare and valuable, and Joaquin is a greedy man."

"The last I knew, the plans were in a closet under the stairs in the leadership pavilion," Gray said. "And the detail I remember best of all was a date, labeled 'day of action' and written alongside a sketch of the bog."

"And there's a tunnel somewhere," Stella said. "He's been working on it for years."

"I see," I said, remembering the day I'd watched him collect moss and disappear. Could I have missed the tunnel? It was clear Joaquin was skilled at covering his tracks. "How long has Joaquin been in power?"

"Way too long," Stella said.

"But why do the others stand for it?" I said, accepting a second helping of grains from Gray.

"Because they're scared," said Ramona. "And they don't want to end up like us. They don't want to lose their families. Besides, their lives are pretty good, for the most part."

"For now," I said. "I guess it all depends on what those plans are for."

Owl hooted above.

"Look at that," Gray said, pointing to Owl. "An owl at dawn."

"That's my companion, Owl. He's reminding me that I should write a letter to my friend," I said. "He'll take it to her back in Harmony Glen. I need to let her know that I'm safe."

Gray handed me a pen and some tree bark, and I wrote to Rapunzel. We had to get to work fast.

26

EUGENE

"Are you coming to the celebration brunch?" I called to Rapunzel from inside the caravan. I had just groomed my goatee, brushed my hair, and splashed my face with cold water. I was looking sharp and was ready to fully enjoy the celebration brunch Joaquin and the village council were throwing in my honor. It was so touching how much this performance meant to the people of Harmony Glen.

I really hoped that Rapunzel realized Cass was okay. She'd just moved on. She'd been really off since we'd left Corona. Harmony Glen was so positive, and Cass was so, well, Cass. Of course she hadn't liked it there. Vardaros would be much better for her. She could wield her weapons and feel more at home. There was no one to shoot arrows at around here. Harmony Glen had zero crime.

As I shaved my cheeks one more time for maximum smoothness, I wondered why Rapunzel didn't see it that way. She was the smartest person I knew, and she always saw the best in everyone. Maybe she saw the best in Cass to the point that she missed the rest of her.

Oh, well. I sighed and added some barber's gel to my hair, giving it an extra-sleek look. Then I tousled it to make it look more Rider-esque. I couldn't let my people down. One last glance in the mirror and I was off.

There was my girl, sitting on a rock with her sketch pad and pencils.

"Blondie, are you coming?" I asked.

"Oh!" She jumped. The frog was sleeping on her shoulder, but her sudden movement sent him leaping onto her head. "You startled me." She looked up at Pascal. "Us, I guess."

"Rapunzel?" She nodded, but she had dark circles under her eyes and a bit of a crazed expression. She always looked beautiful to me, but she didn't appear to be ready to go to a formal occasion. "Are you okay?"

"Yes, I'm better than okay," she said. "Take a look at this!"

She showed me the portrait of us setting out for the road. Only this time, she really looked like herself. Full of life, totally natural, and a spark of joy and adventure in her eye.

"I'm back!" she said. "I mean, as an artist. It turned out that I just needed to focus on one thing at a time."

"I see what you're saying now," I said. "This is wonderful. It's more . . . *you*. Were you up all night doing this?"

She nodded proudly.

"So I guess that means you're not coming to my Flynn Fest brunch at the pavilion? You look like you could use some rest. . . ."

"Oh, I'm coming," she said.

"Really? I'm so glad! You finally get how great this place is?"

"Eugene, Cass is missing," Rapunzel said, standing.

"Because she wanted to leave early," I replied, reaching for her hand.

But Rapunzel was distracted by Owl. He called out from above and then swooped low, dropping a note by her feet.

"Owl!" she exclaimed. "Is Cass okay?"

He hooted and nodded at the note, which was written on tree bark.

"What does it say?" I asked, thinking she would finally get the proof she needed that Cass had gone of her own free will.

Rapunzel's fingers were trembling as she read aloud:

Raps,

Not sure exactly where I am, but I'm alive and okay. I was captured inside of Wolf's studio. I woke up in the woods, but I'm going to use all of my cartography skills to locate myself. I'm with Stella and the other runaways, Gray and Ramona.

"Ramona!" Rapunzel said. "That's who Wolf told me to look for."

Huh. The letter seemed a tad concerning so far, and the name rang a bell. Then I remembered why. "It's also the name in one of the stories missing from the library: *Ramona and the Seven Dragons,*" I said.

Rapunzel kept reading.

None of them wanted to leave Harmony Glen. We're going to find our way back. Owl will help. Until then, you must find a way to get through

*to the people and figure out what Joaquin is up
to. They tell me you must go to the leadership
pavilion and find the plans kept in the closet
under the stairs. Do this AS SOON AS POSSIBLE. It
wasn't always like this! The people have forgotten
who they are. Please help them remember. We can
change everything.*

Cass

Rapunzel gazed up at me with huge eyes. "Do
you believe me now?"

"Um . . ." I was confused. Cass wasn't a liar. But
she'd also been so off-kilter ever since we'd set out
on our journey—so uptight and controlling. And I
didn't want to believe that Harmony Glen was the
terrible place she was convinced it was. There was
still a chance that it wasn't. Maybe it just didn't
float her boat. "I think Cass has become really negative since we left Corona. It's possible it's skewed
her vision and now she's fallen in with a bad crowd
of other negative people who hate Harmony Glen."

"Eugene," Rapunzel said, slightly exasperated.
"This is about something bigger than us."

I couldn't help feeling stung. Lately, it seemed
like nothing was about us. "Ouch."

"I didn't mean that in the way that I think you
thought I meant it," she said, rubbing her eyes with

either frustration or fatigue or both. "I'm really tired, okay?"

"Okay," I said. "I just don't want to jump to any conclusions."

"And I want to protect the people of Harmony Glen, who are living in danger."

A group of children with flowered wreaths on their heads skipped past us, locked arm in arm, waving to me. I looked at Rapunzel and cocked an eyebrow.

"I didn't say they weren't happy," Rapunzel said. "I said they were in danger."

"Happy danger?" I asked.

She nodded, though it looked like it pained her.

"Eugene, I believe this with my whole heart," Rapunzel said.

I looked my love right in the eye and tried as hard as I could to agree with her with *my* whole heart, but I just couldn't. I didn't believe there was anything wrong there. I looked deep into my soul—honestly, I did—and then I gazed at all the joy around me, from the singing birds to the sweet kids to the flourishing trees and the puffy clouds. I just couldn't conjure up the confidence that something terrible was happening there.

Instead, all I felt was sadness that Blondie and I weren't connecting the way we always had in the

past. We usually saw eye to eye, or at least understood each other's points of view. But now it just
seemed like she and Cass were totally against a
place that had been so kind to me. Harmony Glen
had given me a meaningful task, something I'd
been missing ever since we'd left the kingdom. I
was at a loss.

"I promise that I'll keep listening to your argu-
ment," I said. She sighed. "But I'm attending this
ceremony in good faith. And I would really love
for you to stand beside me, inspiring the people
of Harmony Glen the way you do the people of
Corona."

"I'll inspire them," Rapunzel said. "But maybe
just not in the way Joaquin expects."

She left it at that as she began to collect her art
supplies and headed toward the caravan.

"What does that mean, exactly?" I asked, feeling nervous. There was a certain fervor in her
voice that matched the one in Cassandra's earlier.
"Because I'm not sure that stealing documents is
how we want to repay our host, who has treated us
so nicely and is having a brunch in honor of me.
Brunch is such a friendly meal! Some might say
the friendliest meal of all—breakfast and lunch
overcoming *their* differences to come together." I
could tell I was losing her. "I don't know. I'm just

saying revolution might not be the message of appreciation we want to send?"

"Change can be a good thing, Eugene," she said. "And all voices deserve to be heard if they can find the courage to speak. Because they aren't being intimidated. Right? I'm not planning on having a revolution at this celebration, I'm just hoping to gather some information—information that might be hidden away in a small dark room under the staircase of the leadership pavilion. Anyway, I should get ready."

She gave me a peck on the cheek and ducked inside the caravan. I sighed and slumped against a tree. I took three deep breaths to clear my mind, just like Rapunzel did in demanding circumstances. When she emerged from the caravan moments later, looking refreshed, I did feel clearer.

This was my girl—the most amazing person I'd ever met. And she was still coming to my brunch. We just needed to figure things out.

"I'm ready," she said, tucking a flower into her braid.

I took her gently by the shoulders and looked into her eyes.

"Is it just me, or are we not really talking to each other, Rapunzel?" I asked. "It's more like we're talk-ing *past* each other."

Her brow crinkled with frustration. "I'm being as honest with you as I can, but I feel like you're not listening."

Uh-oh. It seemed we were heading back down a bad road.

"Me? I feel like *you're* not listening," I said.

"I'm trying," she said.

"Joaquin is a good leader who's keeping the peace," I said. "Harmony Glen is thriving. I think that Cass has really gotten to you, and that's the problem."

"What?" Rapunzel asked, drawing back. "I'm sorry, Eugene. I love you, but I don't agree. I'm thinking for myself. I think the *problem* is that Harmony Glen has gotten to *you*."

Whoa. "If by *gotten to me* you mean filled me with hope and purpose, then yes, it has," I said, while at the same time wondering how I could feel so sad and despondent as I uttered words like *hope* and *purpose*.

"I guess we'll have to agree to disagree," she said. We stared at each other for a moment, searching each other's eyes for common ground. Finally, she spoke. "Maybe we just need some space."

Her words hit like the sharpest arrow from Cassandra's bow.

"Maybe that's it," I said, though distance was the

last thing I wanted. "I'll see you later. I guess you aren't coming, then?"

"I'm going to this brunch," she said, her eyes starting to fill. "But I'll let you get a head start."

I walked ahead, my heart as heavy as armor.

And in my mind was a small nagging itch. What if Cass was right?

27

RAPUNZEL

I waited for Eugene to be fifty paces ahead before I started down the path to the leadership pavilion, but it broke my heart. I'd been so full of inspiration just an hour earlier. I had finally started to feel more like myself—more confident in my ability to lead and to solve tough problems. And usually after I saw Eugene I felt like a spoonful of honey catching the sunlight before being stirred into tea. So why, I wondered, did I feel like I'd just stepped on the teacup, breaking it into many shards? What exactly was happening with us?

I watched him turn a corner and started on my

way, my sketch pad and pencil tucked into my pocket.

My heart seemed to be traveling one step behind me as I walked, but as much as it hurt, I had to simply accept that our disagreement was temporary. I had to believe in the larger portrait of us.

As I passed a field of wild lavender bending in a soft southern breeze, I wondered if Cass and I were wrong and Eugene was right. Maybe Joaquin was simply the best leader of all time and that's why everyone was so happy. After all, Eugene was a good judge of character—he could spot a rotten apple before anyone else—and he said he felt in his heart that Joaquin wasn't bad.

He was the one who had lived on the streets by his wits and survived on the open road. Cass and I had not. I'd been in a tower for most of my life, and Cass, for all her toughness, had grown up inside Corona's walls. Being on the road was throwing us all for a loop.

I caught a glimpse of Eugene, felt a pinch in my chest at the distance between us, and let him gain a bit more of a lead. As I saw the topiary gardens on my right, the children trimming them with shears to keep the animal shapes in their perfect poses, I remembered Flynn Rider's words about the illusion of perfection. *There's no such thing as flawlessness, and the desire for it belies an emptiness I hope you never know.*

I smiled at Daphne and Molly, accepting their sweet gifts of flowers.

"We love you," Daphne remarked, throwing her arms around my waist.

"Aw, I love you, too," I said.

I knew that when she said "we" she spoke for her sister and herself. I felt a sharp pang for Cassandra—the only sister I had ever known. I thought about Wolf and Stella, who had only had each other to rely upon. As I took in the girls' happy faces, I knew that I needed to get into the room under the staircase at the leadership pavilion.

I smiled and thanked them with a great big hug, and then I continued on my journey. Eugene might have been on the road before, but I had not. I had my own discoveries to make.

"Greetings, Princess," Joaquin said as I entered the pavilion. Out of the corner of my eye, I saw Eugene shaking hands with the village council. My palms were sweating in anticipation. I'd had all the courage in the world when I'd imagined taking the plans, but now that the moment was upon me, my heart was racing.

"Hello," I said and curtsied, hoping that he couldn't see the nervousness in my eyes.

"I hear that your friend Cassandra has decided to leave us early. Is this true?" Joaquin asked as he took my hand in his and bowed to show his respect.

"Unfortunately, yes," I answered. I wanted to rip my hand away and let him know that I was onto him, and I could feel my pulse speed up. *Stay calm*, I told myself. *Remember the goal, and play along until you have the information we need. One thing at a time.*

"Harmony Glen isn't for everyone, and that's okay," Joaquin said, with my hands still in his. And for a lightning-quick moment I felt it—his power of persuasion. It was in the way he looked me in the eye. Though the pavilion was crowded with admirers, it felt for a second like I was the only person in the room. I met his gaze. He continued, "Those with a skeptical nature are usually happier elsewhere. You and Eugene add so much to our community, and we are grateful for your positivity."

"We have been honored to be your guests," I said, standing tall.

His eyes twinkled as he took my arm in his and we walked through the crowd toward the head table. I waved to all the townspeople, who were chatting and smiling, excited for this event. At the same time, I glanced above their heads, turning subtly to check out the spaces behind them, hoping I might see the door to the closet under the staircase. There was no sign of it.

"Are you . . . looking for something?" Joaquin asked. "Is there anything I can help you find?"

"No," I chirped. My voice was oddly high. Was I being too obvious? I coughed. "I'm, ah, just taking in the sight of these wonderful people. I want to see each and every smiling face."

Joaquin nodded as we took our places at the head table. I couldn't tell if he believed me or not. Ahead of us, Eugene was circulating among the people, charming everyone he spoke with.

"As I'm sure you know, Eugene has been an incredible help to us. Because he took over the role of Flynn Rider, I was finally able to dedicate myself to the wellness of this city, and realizing our bigger dreams," Joaquin said as he pulled out a chair for me.

I sat down, wondering how I was ever going to find the closet with Joaquin sitting right next to me!

Joaquin turned to me. "Eugene has really embraced his role as Flynn Rider," he said. "Isn't it wonderful?"

"I do believe that there is no greater good than inspiring people to be their true selves, flaws and all," I replied, continuing to draw on the wisdom of Flynn Rider.

A shadow, as quick as a cloud on a windy March day, passed across his face. But Joaquin recovered quickly—too quickly. Had I given too much away? My throat went dry and I guzzled some lavender lemonade.

"I'm so happy the residents here are receiving us so graciously," I said with my most princessy smile.

"As am I," Joaquin said, matching my expression. "And as for your friend, I hope that she finds her truth without too much danger. I worry for negative sorts like herself."

There was a warning in his voice. I didn't miss it and he knew it.

"She's a great warrior, Joaquin," I said, and I recognized immediately that there was power in simply stating someone's name. "There is no need to worry for her."

When Eugene sat next to me, I offered him an apologetic smile, as if to say, *Even though we don't understand each other right now, I'm still me. And you're still you. And we are still us.* He smiled back, and my heart flipped. I knew, somehow, that we would be okay.

Joaquin tapped his glass with his knife, signaling a speech.

"Eugene Fitzherbert, will you stand up?" Joaquin said. The crowd applauded. "You are such an inspiration to us all."

Eugene rose, basking in the attention. I smiled and clapped, though I realized that with all the focus on him, I had a chance to resume my search for the closet door. My eyes returned to the staircase. One side of it was against the wall, so the only possible entrance was from the area I was staring at, and the wood was smooth and uniform. Where was this closet? I didn't have a lot of time!

"I'm so happy to be here today," Eugene began. "I've never felt so at home as I do here!"

Those words caught me by surprise, diverting my attention from my mission.

More at home here in Harmony Glen than in Corona?

Was that really true? As if he could read my thoughts, he rested a hand on my shoulder, stuttered for a second and added, "I—I guess what I mean is that the people of Harmony Glen have welcomed me—welcomed us—with such warmth and gratitude, I can't help but feel at home among you. As Flynn Rider said, 'Greet adventure with your whole self—the body, mind, and spirit. It's never too late to remember who you really are, and there's no moment better than right now.'"

We weren't entirely lost. He was reaching out to me. We both believed in those words.

"Or as we say here in Harmony Glen, only the now is real," Joaquin interrupted.

"But that's the original quote," Eugene said. "I remembered it the other day. . . ."

He was, in his special Eugene way, challenging Joaquin! I could've kissed him right then and there.

"Our visitors have brought immeasurable joy to Harmony Glen," Joaquin said, changing tactics. "Let us all raise a glass of lavender lemonade to the Coronan couple that has bestowed happiness to our people, allowing your leader to tend to the administrative tasks!"

The crowd cheered. And then Eugene did something I didn't expect. He kept pushing!

"I noticed that one of my favorite stories, *Flynn Rider and the Wild Beasts of Willabee Willows*, was missing from your library," Eugene said. "Luckily, I have it memorized, as I used to tell it to my fellow orphans at night. Why don't I share it now? To get us all ready for tomorrow's performance! Lance, would you join me up here? I need someone to be the bad guys. Actually, I think this will be better out on the lawn. Come on, everyone. Bring your muffins and eggs!"

Everyone clapped. We smiled at each other. He was giving me an opportunity, even though he wasn't sure if I was right. I studied the staircase. I would dash to it as soon as the crowd stood up.

"Um . . . That wasn't what I planned," Joaquin said, his voice threaded with the same uneasy surprise as when he'd discovered me wandering around the leadership pavilion my first day there, when I had been revealed by the mirror on the ceiling. . . . *The mirror on the ceiling!*

I looked up and saw it from the bird's-eye view: a plank on the staircase was slightly larger and lighter than the rest! That had to be it! I delicately covered my mouth with my hand so no one could see me smiling. My heart beat like a drum. Would I be able to investigate unnoticed? I looked at Joaquin, who was focused on his audience with a furrowed brow. It would be hard for him to deny them this when he had no reason to. He sighed and said, "But if the spirit of Flynn Rider has moved you, I shan't get in the way."

Everyone clapped, delighted. Eugene squeezed my shoulder. I placed my hand on his and took a deep breath. This was my moment.

"To the great lawn!" Eugene cried, gesturing outside. The crowd rose to their feet, cheering, and followed him.

"Yay!" I said, cheering on the townspeople as they left the pavilion.

"Aren't you coming?" Joaquin asked.

"Of course," I said. "I'm just going to grab an extra muffin from the kitchen."

"I'll send someone to get one for you," he said.

"Nonsense. I've heard this story before, but the townspeople haven't," I said. "I could never ask one of them to miss this."

"Very well," Joaquin said, turning to go. "I'll see you soon."

As I watched him leave, my heart felt like a bull-frog in my throat. Joaquin was going to be waiting for me, so I'd have to be as fast as I'd ever been! Wrapping my hair around a ceiling beam, I flew across the room, landing on the staircase. I loosened the plank. The wood gave way, revealing an opening just big enough for me to slip inside. I lowered myself down.

It was dark, but it only took a moment of feeling around to discover a lantern. Once it was lit, it became clear this was a private office—complete with a tidy little desk and a wooden stool.

And right on the desk was a notebook labeled *Flynn Rider Festival Plans*. Hoping Eugene would draw out his story for as long as he could, I opened the notebook and began to read.

28
CASSANDRA

Joaquin and the village council were using the Flynn Rider Festival as the designated time to put their new plan—whatever it was—into place, that much was clear. They thought they'd rooted out the potential rebels, Stella being the last one and the person with the most information.

But then I'd shown up. They hadn't seen me coming. Obviously, Joaquin had thought he could distract me by casting me as a stupid tree in the play, but he was wrong. I'd been a wrench in his plan, and I was just getting started.

I didn't want to be separated from Rapunzel for much longer. We had work to do, and our detour to Harmony Glen had lasted long enough. The mystery of the rocks wasn't going to solve itself, and the longer we took to save the village, the more time was lost from our true mission.

But now, more than ever, it was clear Raps had been right. We couldn't leave without helping the people of Harmony Glen. I'd gotten all the information I possibly could from this group. Now I had to convince them to fight back. After that, I was going to have to guide us back to Harmony Glen. And finally, Rapunzel and I had to wake the entire town to the reality they seemed so intent on denying.

Oh, yeah, *and* I had to do it all in twenty-four hours, because the Flynn Rider Festival was the next day. Yet I could see in this group's eyes the real fear they had about returning to the village.

"We need to get back there before the ceremony," I said.

"Cassandra, we don't know the way," Gray said.

"I'm a skilled cartographer," I explained. "In a few hours, I should be able to head us in the right direction. Is there some tree bark I can use as paper?"

"I'll find some," Stella said.

"What about the waterfall?" Ramona asked. "How will we ever cross it?"

"There has to be a way," I said. "Or the masked person would not have been able to get us here."

Stella returned with the supplies and I made a preliminary sketch. I didn't have any of my other maps with me, so I'd have to rely on my memory and skill. This was an especially difficult task because the modern maps I'd been studying didn't have Harmony Glen on them. My talent was surely going to be put to the test.

"The falls are so steep," Gray said. "We would all perish!"

"You can't live like this forever, out here in the woods," I said. "Where's your courage?"

I couldn't believe it, but I found myself wishing Gray had a little more of Eugene's bravery and pluck in him.

"What if we try and then fail?" Gray asked. "We'll be worse off than we are now. They could split us up."

Was that possible?

"We need our families and they need us. It's worth the risk," Stella said.

"She's right," Ramona said, planting her stick in the ground. "We deserve to live there, and to tell our stories just as my grandfather did."

Gray nodded.

Stella had the words the others needed to be fully convinced. I wondered, perhaps for the first time in my life, if I needed to listen more. Ugh.

This had been my error. I'd tried to control our journey when I'd needed to cooperate more. That was an essential part of being a good warrior, and it was something I'd been missing lately. I guess I'd been too caught up in the mission, and in my own responsibilities. I hadn't trusted anyone—Eugene, even Raps—to help out on the road. Even though it was clear they—*especially* Raps—were more than capable of doing so.

Just then, as if reading my thoughts, Owl arrived with a letter from Rapunzel.

I found the plans! I didn't want to alert Joaquin to their absence, so I had to read them as quickly as possible. They were sketches of a tunnel to the bog and tools to remove the moss.

"Yes, that's what I saw!" Gray interrupted. "Keep reading!"

I also saw sketches that show he will close the village's borders, locking them forever. It's all supposed to happen tomorrow—Flynn Rider Day. I didn't have much time, but clearly he wants to remove the blue moss from the bog and then lock the gates to Harmony Glen permanently—both entrances. It looks like he

*has someone ready to help him sell the moss
outside of the village. Joaquin will be the only
one allowed to come and go as he pleases.*

"He told us he was revealing a new emblem on
Flynn Rider Day, but it looks like he plans on locking the place up instead," I said. "Forever."

"That blue moss is invaluable. When it reaches
a high heat, it forms the strongest metal known
to humankind," Stella said. "The ancient people of
Harmony Glen used it to make crafts." She held up
the bright blue metal piece from her studio.

"And now he's going to sell it to some horrible
thief, destroying our home," Ramona said.

"When do we leave?" Gray asked.

"As soon as possible," Ramona said.

Then they all looked at me.

29

RAPUNZEL

After I wrote the letter to Cass, I knew more than ever I had to get through to the people of Harmony Glen. I was going to do it the only way I knew how: through art. And I had to do it before the next day—before the Flynn Rider Festival.

"We're going to do things a little bit differently today," I told my students, who had gathered in our usual spot. They arrived prepared with their easels and paintbrushes. "Instead of continuing to work on the portraits Joaquin asked for, we're going to focus on one part of ourselves and see what we learn!"

I was so eager to share my own discovery with

them, and I couldn't wait to see what each person found special about him or herself. I felt the excitement bubbling up inside me, but a worried expression on Daphne's face made me pause. And quiet Edmond furrowed his brow.

"But aren't we supposed to be drawing our portraits in exactly the same style as Flynn Rider's famous picture?" Molly asked. Others looked concerned and grave as well.

"Yes," I said, taking a deep breath. "It's what we're *supposed* to do, but art isn't really about following instructions or doing what you're told. It's about finding your own voice."

"I'm sorry," Carole the musician said, raising her hand. "I don't follow."

Wolf looked a little pale.

"Let's back up a little bit," I said with an encouraging smile. Words were not going to be enough. I needed to *show* them what I meant. I opened my sketchbook to my original portrait and displayed it.

"This was my first attempt at a self-portrait," I said.

"It's lovely!" Daphne exclaimed.

"You know what?" I said as I looked out at them all seated in neat rows. "I think you're a little far away. How about you take your notebooks off of the easels and come sit here on the ground with me. Then you'll really be able to see what I'm talking about. And if you feel like it, take off your shoes or let down your hair, or do whatever you need to do to feel comfortable."

"Take off our shoes?" Molly said. "But we're outside!"

"Even better," I said.

"We aren't supposed to let down our hair!" Daphne said.

"Today we're artists," I said. "And artists need to be free."

Tentatively, my students slipped off their shoes or removed their vests. I gestured for them to join me on the soft earth. As they approached, I saw a glimmer in their eyes, like I really had their attention. They were listening. I showed them the portrait I had started on our journey.

"What do you notice about this picture?" I asked.

"Your lines are well drawn and graceful," Wolf said.

"It looks just like you," Grace added.

"It would be perfect for the portrait wall," Molly said.

"Thank you," I said. "Now tell me what you think of this one." I turned the page to the picture of my feet. I felt them draw closer to me. Molly giggled. Daphne did, too.

"The first picture looked like you, but this one *feels* like you," Wolf said.

"Exactly!" I said. He'd found just the right words. "I didn't want to draw a picture that simply looked like me, because even though that can be neat, it's not why I love art. Art makes me *feel*."

"How did you do it?" Wolf asked.

"I decided to focus on one detail," I said, meeting Wolf's eyes as I repeated the wisdom he had shared with me. "In changing something that might seem small and irrelevant, the whole picture changed."

"Why'd you choose your feet?" Molly asked as she pulled on her corkscrew curls.

"Yeah," Daphne said. "The thing that's so different and special about you is your hair, right?"

"My hair is definitely unique," I said. "But my feet have always gotten me where I need to go. They touch the ground in all seasons. They're kind of funny." I wiggled my toes. "They don't like shoes, and they're what keeps me connected to the earth. I love the feeling of the ground beneath them as I run through fields or climb a tree. I like how flexible they are. They have character. They're really strong. And they have all kinds of interesting lines and scratches from being so close to the earth all the time. When I looked at them, really looked at them, they told a story about me that I wanted to share. Is there a part of you that tells a story about your life?"

"My hands," quiet Edmond said. I'd never heard him speak before, and his voice was so low I had to listen well.

"Great!" I said. "Why is that?"

"When I was young, even younger than you, Princess, I helped my grandfather build a house. He was a master craftsman. We made cabinets together with beautiful engravings. Those are some of my favorite memories. Though, of course, I just build things according to plan now. I still remember what it was like to create my own plans and then bring them to life with my hands."

"Edmond, that's so lovely! I can't wait to see your work," I said. He went to his easel and began.

"I'm going to draw my hair," Daphne said.

"Me too," Molly said.

"I guess that means you'll have to take out those buns!" I said. Grins spread across their faces and their eyes lit up.

"Our curls are wild," Molly said as Daphne removed the pins and elastics from her hair.

"They're bouncy and funny," Daphne replied. "Kind of like us!"

"Boing!" Molly said as she pulled a curl taut and then let it spring back to her head. Then she jumped as though she were a curl herself. Daphne giggled.

"No one said art had to be serious," I said. I couldn't help laughing along with them as they hopped back to their easels like two rabbits. Their curls bounced along with them.

"I'm going to draw my ears," Carole said as she touched them with her long fingers.

"I'd love to hear why," I said.

"I used to love to write and play my own music, not just the tunes for Evensing. I would listen to nature for inspiration," Carole said. "But I'd love to have some sort of model. . . ."

"It's a good thing I brought some mirrors," I said, handing her one. She held it to her face and turned to the side. The corners of her mouth turned up as she studied her ear.

Other students seemed to be inspired by those who had spoken up. They walked or ran back to their easels. Some took mirrors, others did not.

"Remember to draw what you see, not what you want to see," I reminded them.

Wolf stood in front of his easel, frowning.

"What is it, Wolf?" I asked. "What part of you are you going to draw?"

"I'm not going to draw anything," he said.

"Wolf, why not?" I asked.

"I don't know where to start. I don't have a story," he said.

"Of course you have a story. It was your story that helped me realize this truth," I said.

"I wasn't supposed to tell you that, Rapunzel," he whispered.

"But you did. And I loved hearing about Stella." Wolf's eyes widened at my mention of her name. "She's your family. And there's nothing more important than family." I lowered my voice. "And I happen to know that she's safe, and if everything goes well, you'll see her again—soon."

Wolf's eyes widened with hope and surprise. Then he frowned and looked away, as if just realizing something.

"I should go," Wolf said, suddenly clamming up.

"Please stay," I said. "Your story is important."

But it was too late. He placed his pencil on the easel and walked toward the path. My heart sank as I watched him disappear behind the topiary trees.

As the afternoon progressed, the art class seemed to become more than a lesson. The students' eyes lit up. There was laughter. Carole began humming to herself. Edmond created a border around his portrait, which he told me was the same design he'd engraved on those cabinets he'd built with his grandfather. Daphne and Molly had filled their pages with squiggles and loops. If they hadn't told me they were drawing hair, I never would have known. But there was endless joy in their rambunctious circles and curlicues.

"What is going on here?" Joaquin startled me as I peered over Edmond's shoulder. He was definitely light on his feet. "Tell me what your class is doing, Rapunzel."

Joaquin was smiling, but his face was stiff, and despite his measured voice, his eyes were flashing with anger.

"Self-portraits," I said.

"These are not the self-portraits I requested," Joaquin said.

"You mean the copies of that picture of Flynn Rider?" I asked.

"Of course that's what I mean. That picture is so sunny," Joaquin said. He looked at Molly and Daphne's work. "This is, well, unsettling."

"That's not what I see when I look at this. I see . . . fun," I said.

I could feel my students' fear, and was surprised to notice that my own hands were sweating. But I was determined to be brave. I could do this. I could stand my ground. My students needed to know that there was more than one way to respond to Joaquin—that fear was a thread strung between two people. Joaquin held up one end through his subtle intimidation, but they held up the other side of it by being afraid. They played a part in granting Joaquin his power. I inhaled deeply and smiled.

"It's just a fun exercise," I said. "And don't you think the diversity will add to the beauty of the mural?"

"Dear Princess," Joaquin said. "You are from another land."

"Corona is not so very far away," I said.

"And yet, the miles may as well be oceans. May I speak with you in private?" he asked.

"Of course," I answered. I could feel the weight of my students' gazes on us.

Joaquin walked several paces away. He gestured for me to join him. I faced my students, doing my very best to communicate levity and cheer, and said, "I'll just be a minute, artists. Continue with your pictures!" They remained frozen in place, but I smiled at them and then stepped lightly toward Joaquin.

"I wouldn't dare correct you or, heaven forbid, reprimand you," Joaquin said with his warmest smile. "You are, after all, a princess."

"I am," I replied with my sweetest smile.

Joaquin laughed along with me. I stole a quick glance at my students. They weren't even chatting among themselves.

"But even still—"

"Do you know where Cassandra is?" I asked, interrupting him.

"Your friend didn't like it here." Joaquin lowered his voice even more. He stroked his goatee. I supposed this was to signal a shift into a serious discussion. "She left. This is a free land."

That wasn't how I'd describe the way Joaquin ran Harmony Glen.

"I trust that you understand this," he continued.

"Of course. Corona is a free land as well," I said.

"And I also trust that you are simply abiding by the laws of your kingdom?"

"Yes," I said. "The laws of Corona were well thought out by its founders and benefit all of its citizens."

"Well . . . as the king sees fit," Joaquin said.

"Excuse me?" I said.

"Isn't it lovely that we don't even need laws here in Harmony Glen?" Joaquin answered, gesturing to the lavender fields as though they bloomed as a result of his leadership. Then he changed the subject very quickly, as if turning a page. "Everyone here is well taken care of and happy, and I believe that's due to our philosophy of living. I wish I could say the same for Corona, which has fallen into disrepair." Before I could respond, Joaquin raised his voice to be overheard by the others and pronounced, "We all do what's best for the greater good at all times." Without so much as blinking, Joaquin squared his shoulders and spoke up a little louder, transitioning into a speech as he faced my students. "Everyone, please listen up. This dear princess doesn't know our culture, and without meaning to—we know that, as Coronan royalty, her intentions would never be less than pure—she has set you on a path to unhappiness. My disappointment is not with her. How could I ever be disappointed in a princess?"

"Um, but I asked them to follow my example," I said, seeing where this was headed. "So you *should* blame me."

"Never," Joaquin said. "You are royalty. And I am but a commoner, leading his humble flock to the small happiness that is available to those without your distinguished lineage."

He bowed. I felt nauseous. He was so full of lies. He was a bully with a secret plan!

"Wait, no!" I stammered, trying to regain my ground. I'd played right into his hand.

"It's you—my people—who I am disappointed in," he continued. I watched helplessly as shame washed over their faces. Carole's pencil dropped to the ground. Molly and Daphne tucked their curls back under their bonnets. Edmond shoved his hands in his pockets. "You knew what was best for Harmony Glen, but you didn't follow the path. And so I must remove two stars on the chart from every pupil who has participated in this event."

"Just take away *my* stars!" I exclaimed.

"I wouldn't dream of it," Joaquin said with a bow. "I humble myself in your presence."

Always be strategic, I thought as I channeled Cass and her warrior wisdom.

"Thank you," I said, bowing in front of Joaquin and then—as quickly as possible—meeting my students' eyes.

Get the work, a voice inside of me said.

"I apologize for leading you down this path," I began as I walked among them, picking up the portraits and holding them against my chest. Joaquin looked on, his mouth twitching with satisfaction. "And I take it upon myself to remove this art from your vision—though, personally, I love it!" I couldn't help myself. "But as Joaquin said, I'm just an interloper here."

That's when I saw Owl, circling above.

"We'll try again tomorrow, only this time we'll get right back to work on the portraits Joaquin described," I said.

Molly looked up at me, perplexed. Daphne's eyes were filled with tears, though she had managed to keep them from spilling over.

"So we will meet again, and we will finish what Joaquin requests," I said, tearing the last sheet of paper off Edmond's easel. "Though once an artist has awakened, it is impossible to return fully to sleep."

As soon as I was alone, I read the note from Cassandra that Owl had brought in his beak.

You must teach the people to rise up against Joaquin. There are only four of us out here in the woods. The entire community must act together. Do what you were born to do. Lead.

I'm sorry I tried to control so much of the trip before. I just wanted to make sure you'd be okay. But I know you've got this.

Cass

30
CASSANDRA

That evening, the "runaways" and I sat around the fire, plotting how to get back to Harmony Glen. We feasted on cooked berries and mushrooms as big as dinner plates.

"We know Owl can get there in a few hours," I said. "So if we leave early we should be able to make it there by dawn. We know the waterfall could be deadly, but there must be another way—a hidden way. We just need to find it. What can you tell me about this landscape?"

I filled in my map as the group told me everything they knew about these woods, like where the forest thickened and where it gave way to fields. I asked where the river bent and where it tended to swell. Stella described the sand and soil, Gray told me about the vegetation in expert detail, and Ramona recounted the wildlife she'd seen in her many weeks there and where she thought the animals fished. I asked where each of them had found themselves after they'd awakened and discovered they'd been captured and removed from Harmony Glen. I focused on each detail individually, just as Raps would when working on a painting.

"Get some sleep," I told the others. "Even if it's just a few hours. We'll need our strength. Meanwhile, I'll be testing out my work."

"Use this torch I've fashioned," Stella said, handing me a branch of slow-burning wood.

With Owl flying nearby, darting ahead and circling back, I attempted various routes. I used a stick as I walked, testing all surfaces for weakness— possible entry to an underground passage. That was the one way I knew for certain we could have been brought there without having to cross the falls.

I knew from my cartography studies that the current near waterfall drop-offs could be so powerful that even the best swimmers would be at risk if they tried to cross the river there. Any significant current was dangerous, mysterious, and unknowable. Obviously, whoever transported us had used an alternate route.

When I reached the edge of the falls, I searched for any method of crossing, but the drop-off was steep, a hundred feet at least. It would have been impossible.

"Any luck?" Gray asked when I returned to camp from my fourth attempt. He had obviously been unable to sleep.

"No," I said.

"I thought so," Gray said.

"I'm not giving up," I told him.

"Are we not going to get back?" Stella asked.

"Is anyone sleeping?" I asked.

"Nope," Ramona said.

"I guess we'll all be relying on adrenaline," I said. "And yes, we'll get back. I just need to find a way to think about this. Is there any place to swim nearby?"

"We're trying to get back to our families and you want to go for a night swim?" Gray asked. "That hardly seems like a good use of time."

"It's a strategy," I said. I was getting a little tired of Gray's constant doubting of me. "The water clears the mind."

Finally, Stella spoke. "There's a swimming hole

about two hundred feet past the cluster of oak trees."

"Thank you," I said. I rolled up my tree bark map and walked in that direction. Was I actually helping these people? Would I ever be able to get them back to their families? And what about me? Was I stuck out there with them? I had to get back to Rapunzel and our mission. We were already behind schedule.

I'd promised the king, the queen, and my father that I would be a stellar lady-in-waiting, so how had I found myself stuck in the woods our first week outside the walls of Corona?

As I kicked off my shoes and dipped in my toe, I gasped at the cold temperature of the water. There was no doubt this swimming hole had formed as a result of the runoff from the waterfall. I could hear the roar of the falls in the distance like a continuous ocean wave. I jumped in. It was freezing but refreshing.

The strangest thing happened as I plunged into the dark depths. A line from Hook Foot's solo in that stupid Flynn Rider play surfaced in my mind. *When the path is blocked, find your wings, and fly, fly, fly.* It was during this scene that Eugene flew across the audience on a vine. A vine! Of course. I laughed underwater. Raps would have immediately thought of that because of her hair.

When I emerged from the ice-cold water and pulled myself to shore, I looked up. The branches were tall and long vines hung down. I pulled my garments on, grabbed Stella's handmade torch, and continued to explore. I didn't have an answer yet, but I was onto something: if we couldn't go under it, and we couldn't go through it, we'd have to go over it. Ramona, Stella, and Gray would catch on quickly. And if they didn't, well, I *was* a Fitness for Fun instructor.

The moonlight revealed a tiny island in the reservoir that formed at the bottom of the falls. If I could make it to the island with the vine, perhaps there was a crossing. As a cartographer, I knew sometimes the very next step was all I was allowed to see in advance. I couldn't plan this out like one of my itineraries. I would have to take it one step at a time.

I got a good grip on a vine and a great running start, figuring that if I didn't make it to the next bit of land, I could always swing back.

But I did make it, taking care not to let go of the vine when I touched ground. And what I found there took my breath away: it was a log that had been hollowed out and transformed into a canoe.

31

RAPUNZEL

My heart was still racing a good ten minutes after Joaquin had left.

"You can still stay here and draw!" I told my students, though none of them would make eye contact with me. Some of them nodded, but most of them simply stared at the ground and collected their supplies, dutifully organizing the pencils, charcoal, and erasers. "You did great work today! I'm so proud of you!"

"Princess," Molly whispered as she tugged on my sleeve. I crouched so that I was eye level with her. "We all lost *two stars*."

"I don't know if that's ever happened before.

I mean, for just one incident," Edmond added.

I nodded as the gravity of the situation landed.

"Okay," I said, wishing there was something I could do to show them that it didn't matter what this one person—Joaquin—thought. They were more than just his opinion of them. I felt sick as I realized this was all because of me. They'd only been following my directions. "I'll go talk to him. I am a princess after all."

"Don't!" Molly said, and then clasped her hand over her mouth.

"What if you make it worse?" Grace asked. "What if we lose yet another star?" At this suggestion, Molly gasped. Daphne squeezed her hand and then looked at me pleadingly. "Please, Princess, don't say anything."

"Oh . . . okay," I relented.

"Promise us," Molly said. Daphne's watchful eyes focused on me as she squeezed her sister's hand.

"I promise," I said.

The twins held hands and walked away.

Again, I found myself questioning my actions. I knew in my heart that I'd been trying to do the right thing, but as I watched them bow their heads, collect their supplies, and walk toward their homes, I wondered if I had, in reality, put them in harm's way. After all, we weren't in Corona. I was a guest in this land.

I waited until they were out of sight to review their sketches. The sun shone high and brilliant in the cloudless bright blue sky, and Pascal rested on my shoulder. I laid out their pictures, holding down the corners of the paper with stones. I stood back and gasped.

They were beautiful!

From the twins' hair, to Edmond's designs, to Carole's abstract interpretations of music, these drawings had not only life, but also love in them.

Here was a kneecap, drawn in such exquisite detail I almost squealed!

Here was a mouth, smirking with comedic delight!

Here was a man's chest, with the shape of his actual heart outlined ever so faintly and yet quite prominently, the contrast of the lines between his outer and inner body distinct and important.

Oh! And here was a back! I wondered how the artist had accomplished such a feat. The back had impressive muscles and was clad in a woman's attire, making it clear this belonged to a lady who worked the fields.

I squinted my eyes and stared toward the sun.

This was not a mistake, the sun seemed to say. *You have not steered them wrong.*

I remembered what I'd read of my mother's journal—that she, too, had worked inside the walls of cities with difficult rulers. I remembered that she had persisted. She had listened to her own inner wisdom. As I sat on the hillside with the sun on my shoulders, this gave me strength. I knew I must listen to my own inner wisdom as well. I let the moment fill me up.

I was hardly alone in having inner wisdom. Each one of these students had inner wisdom, too. How else would they have been able to draw those parts of themselves? How else would they have known exactly what to draw? They had been separated from their own self-knowledge through oppression, yes. But it was still there. They just needed to be reminded of it! And they needed to connect with it before tomorrow, when Joaquin was planning on closing the walls of the city and turning these people into an army of automatons.

Stories save people, I thought. *The Author knew that! That's what this whole city is founded upon. The people here just need to remember themselves.*

I tore off several pages of my sketch pad and wrote notes to each of my students. I used Eugene's favorite Flynn Rider quote, the one he'd introduced in full at the banquet.

"It's never too late to remember who you really are. Why not right now?" Meet me at the border wall, and bring all the paint you can find.

Later, when I was back at the caravan and the sun began to lower in the sky, I knew it was time to take action. From our camp I could hear the band warming up. Evensing was going to begin soon. I tucked the notes into my pockets and rushed up the path to the town square.

As the songs began that night I stepped right into place. By now I knew the dances by heart. Eugene was my first partner.

"Are you okay?" Eugene asked.

"Yes," I answered. "Thank you for the opportunity today."

"You deserve the chance to follow your calling, even if it's different from mine," he said. "I thought maybe when you saw there was nothing sinister going on, it would even help you get to love this place as much as I do." I stepped out of line a bit, and Eugene pulled me back into the circle. "We promenade now!" he whispered.

"Oh, yeah! Thanks!" I said, taking his hands in

mine. I knew we only had a few minutes left, and I owed it to him to be honest. Also, it was my heart's desire to speak openly with him. *He isn't Flynn Rider—especially not Harmony Glen's version of Flynn Rider. He's Eugene!*

"I love the people here," I said.

"I know!" Eugene answered as we moved to the music.

"But I know Joaquin is up to no good," I said. "I found plans. Bad ones."

"But how can you be sure . . . ?"

"Eugene, the people I have loved getting to know—and you have, too—deserve better."

"Huh?" Eugene said.

"Trust me," I replied.

He paled. There was no time to talk about it more. Carole was setting the beat as steadily and swiftly as ever. One more bow to Eugene and it was time to change partners.

To my relief, Wolf was my next partner. I pulled the note from my pocket and pressed it into his palm as we joined hands and danced in a circle.

"What's this?" he asked.

"An important message," I said. "And don't forget to tell your friends."

I looked up at the moon and saw Owl circling. There was a break between the fifth and sixth

dance. That's when I would give him my last letter to Cass. I broke hands with Wolf ever so briefly
and held my arm up to the lowering sun, hoping
Owl would know, somehow, that I was signaling
to him.

32

CASSANDRA

O wl, ever the dutiful soldier, delivered Raps's message just as the moon rose over the campsite. Now was the time to reveal my discovery—as well as the danger that came with it.

"What does it say?" Stella asked.

"Wolf is well," I said. "He earned two stars this evening." Stella closed her eyes and sighed with relief. "But we need to move quickly. Rapunzel's plan is for all of the people of Harmony Glen to meet at the border wall at dawn. Instead of portraits of Flynn Rider, they will protest with art, showing Joaquin they will not simply do whatever he asks, just because he asks them."

I led the group to the tall tree with the hanging vines. This, of course, was just the beginning.

"We're going to have to pull a real Flynn Rider move here. It's also a Rapunzel move, but you don't know her well enough to get that yet," I said.

"What exactly do you mean?" Ramona asked.

"She means we're going to have to swing," Stella said, not looking entirely unhappy at the prospect.

"All the way across the waterfall?" Gray said.

"'When the path is blocked, find your wings, and fly, fly, fly,'" I muttered under my breath.

"'*When the path is blocked,*'" Ramona sang with perfect pitch, picking up the evidently familiar song and running with it. Stella joined in, adding harmony. "'*Find your wings, and fly, fly, fly.*'"

"What you're going to do is get a good grip," I instructed. "And then a huge running start. Because of centripetal force, you'll come right back in this direction if you don't make it there. We'll catch you."

"I'm ready," Ramona said.

"What are we going to do when we reach the island?" Gray asked.

"There's a boat there. It's crafted to fit through the narrow passageway behind the next set of falls," I said.

I took Rapunzel's note from my pocket and said, "Rapunzel writes, 'Be here before dawn, at the village limit. I have an army of artists and they are ready to speak the truth, but nothing will motivate them more than the faces of their family. They must return to speak of the wisdom they have learned.'

"All right," I said, rubbing my hands together. "Who's ready to swing?"

The others swung across the waterfalls like total pros. Raps would have been proud. And after we all got to the small island, I showed them the boat carved from the log. Stella paled.

"What's wrong?" I asked.

"Wolf is a boat builder—at least he was before the storm. This looks like his work. Someone must have stolen it from him. I hate the thought."

"I understand," I replied. "Let the fact that you'll soon be with him give you courage."

Stella nodded. Ramona hugged her.

"And you're sure you have a clear idea of where we are headed?" Gray asked.

"We stay as close to the land as possible," I said. "According to my map, sticking to the shore will bring us to the border of Harmony Glen by morning."

Gray motioned for the makeshift map on the piece of bark and I handed it over to him.

"There will be eddies," Gray said.

"So, powerful whirlpools?" I asked.

"Yes, but if we work together, if we stay in constant communication, we will get to the other side. Obviously, our captor has done this before us many times."

"Four, at least," I said.

"And what do you predict after that?" Stella asked. "What does the road look like from there?"

"I can't say," I answered. "We'll have to work together. I'm going to need your knowledge of the landscape in these parts to navigate us with efficiency. But we won't be alone." I pointed to a branch above, where Owl was resting. He uttered a single resounding hoot. "If there are any other deviations, any unforeseen drop-offs beyond the one we already know about, he will tell me."

The air was sweet and dark. The moon was full and bright. Owl hooted again, this time in three short bursts.

"It's time to go," I said.

Together, the runaways and I hoisted the log boat and gently dropped it in the river. Suddenly, the hollowed-out tree looked so delicate. Was it truly hearty enough to carry all of us? Gray stepped in and it sank an inch more than I wanted it to. I tried to muffle my gasp.

"Current's strong," Gray said.

"We're stronger," Stella answered as she climbed aboard. "Our love for our families will guide us."

The runaways cheered. I joined them, of course. But with each body, the fragile vessel sank an important inch lower. I almost hesitated climbing aboard. But I knew if they detected fear in my eyes, we'd never get to Harmony Glen.

"Grab your oars," I said as I pushed off from the riverbank. We'd have to work together, but we'd make it. "We're going home."

The boat rocked, and not a little river water sloshed inside.

"Bail," I said, handing a bucket to Stella.

Her brow creased with anxiety, but she obliged, removing the water in bucket increments as the rest of us paddled onward. She paused, wiping sweat from her brow, and then got right back to it.

The runaways were lean and strong from living in the wilderness. We made it through the calmer waters more quickly than I'd hoped. Gray knew river patterns well and was deft at avoiding eddies.

We were in new territory when we approached the second set of falls. Gray remained a steady oarsman, but Ramona began to panic. Up close the falls were as loud as a stadium full of people, and the mist was so thick it might as well have been rain.

"Left oar," I called, guiding us closer to the mountain and away from the drop-off. "Left! Left!" I exhaled as we veered away from the one-hundred-foot falls. I looked up to Owl, who maintained his flight path. All signs seemed to indicate that we could do this. Nevertheless, I hoped they were all good swimmers.

33

RAPUNZEL

I couldn't sleep a wink, so I was wide-awake when Owl returned with the note from Cass that read: *We're on our way.*

We're ready, I thought.

After trying for another hour to get some sleep, I decided I needed to simply embrace the thrill of the moment and make my way to the border wall, where the star banner hung and only hours before I'd been dancing to the Evensing music. I still didn't like being without Cass, but I took heart in the thought that she was bravely leading the runaways back to Harmony Glen, where they would soon be reunited with their loved ones. *Wolf will be so happy to see Stella*, I thought.

I was so relieved knowing he wouldn't feel alone for much longer.

In the quiet of the predawn hour, I changed out of my nightclothes and into my dress. Pascal, who hadn't been able to sleep, either, hopped up on my shoulder, and I gathered all the paint that I had in my bag. Then we were off.

Well, for a moment we were. Lance's snoring coming from the boys' caravan stopped me in my tracks. I had to cover my mouth to hide my giggles. Of course, my thoughts went quickly to poor Eugene, who probably couldn't sleep, either, with all that racket. It didn't feel right to be on a mission without him, the love of my life. I looked up at Pascal, who nodded.

I threw a pebble at the window that was above Eugene's bed in the boys' wagon. If he would only listen, *really* listen, he would be by my side on this. I knew it. There was no response, so I threw a few more pebbles. Okay, maybe they were rocks, but I didn't toss them forcefully enough to break any glass.

At last I heard some movement! Eugene's fingers pried open the window.

"Blondie?" Eugene said.

"Hi!" I said. It didn't matter what the hour was, Eugene was always adorable to me.

"What time is it?" he asked. "Shouldn't you, er . . . we all still be peacefully asleep . . . ? Don't tell anyone this, but I kind of rely on my beauty sleep."

I couldn't help smiling. His charm hadn't faded a bit.

"It's happening, Eugene," I said.

"What?" he asked, a shadow darkening his already tired face.

"If everything has worked out as I hoped, I'm meeting my students and their families at the border wall. We're going to paint a mural."

"You really believe in this, don't you?" he asked.

I nodded. "I want you to come with me. I want you to stand by my side. Will you?" I asked.

For a moment it felt as though the whole world were hanging in the air between us.

"I need to think about it," he said.

I frowned. "Think fast. Joaquin's plans will crush the people's spirits unless we can stop it. You're going to have to choose sides, Eugene."

His mouth opened but he seemed unable to speak. "I want to support you in all that you do," he began. My eyes widened. "But . . ." His brow furrowed as his voice trailed off.

"You know where to find me," I said, too hurt to say anything else. I turned around, holding my

breath so I wouldn.
town center.

My heart was poundi.
the rest of my body could
have tears in my eyes whe..
They needed to know that I was
fident as ever.

"Rapunzel," a voice called from
turned and saw Molly and Daphne e.
one handle of a bag of paint.

"We took it from the community project..
Daphne said.

"I hope that's not stealing," I said with grit.
teeth. I was, after all, trying to be a role model here.

"What could be a more important project for the
community?" said Carole, who had appeared on
the path behind them. She was also carrying a bag
of paint. "That's what I told myself when I brought
these supplies from the music hall!"

"You're right," I said. "There's nothing more
important than this."

"Princess, were you crying?" Molly asked, gently
touching my damp cheek.

"I was," I said, deciding it was best to be honest,
especially with kids. They always knew the truth
anyway.

?" Ramona asked. "Did someone hurt you?"

I said. "My heart is aching a little."

we making a mistake?" Molly asked.

o," Carole answered, even before I could.

he's right," I said, and I gave the twins a
eeze. "Letting a few tears fall, having your
art break a little, that doesn't mean you're not
doing the right thing. In fact, sometimes that's
part of the deal."

"We love you," Molly said, hugging me tight. I
hugged her right back. In the very same moment
I hoped with my whole self that Eugene would
understand what was at stake, and that he was on
the path behind me.

I held my breath and checked to see if he was
there. Only the lavender, gracefully swaying in the
early morning breeze, waved back at me.

"Come on," I said. "Let's go. We have important
work to do."

"Yes, we do," Carole said. "All of us."

Eugene might not have been there, but the rest
of my art class was—along with all their friends
and family. At least half the town was going to
participate! My heart filled with hope and joy as I
relieved the twins' burden, taking the bag of paint
in my arms and then holding Molly's hand.

"You lead the way," I said to Carole. She nodded and charged onward.

I was planning to join the march as soon as I spotted Wolf, but to my disappointment, he didn't appear. Neither did Eugene. When the last of the portrait students and their families had passed by us, Molly gazed up at me. I was still looking, hoping, wondering.

"What are we waiting for?" she asked.

"Nothing," I said. "Come on, let's go change the world!"

"Change the pictures that you have here. Instead of these portraits, paint the picture that you see of yourself in your heart!" I announced when we arrived at the wall.

I gulped when I saw the lock already on the northern entrance, and I was guessing there was one on the southern gate, too. Joaquin's plan was underway. I had to keep this to myself—for now. My instincts told me it'd be much more powerful to inspire the people than to alarm them. It was time to lead by example.

I had to do what I'd instructed the students to. If I was going to be true to my word—and I'd promised myself I would be—that meant that I had to draw exactly what I saw in my own beating heart. I found an empty spot on the wall and painted myself with Eugene. I didn't render him as Flynn Rider. Instead, I painted the man I knew. I recreated his kind smile and his sparkling eyes when he talked to me—his listening and giving eyes. I painted myself standing next to him and tried to communicate through color, line, and texture how it felt to be heard. I dabbed my brush in a shade of peony and turned one corner of my mouth upward. Sometimes a half smile portrayed the "I really know you" feeling better than a full smile. I was about to add some finishing touches when I felt an arm on my shoulder.

I was so involved in my art that I took a moment to respond.

"Yes?" I asked. I turned, expecting to find one of my dear students, but instead it was Eugene himself.

"You're here," I said.

"I wouldn't miss it," he said, and we embraced.

"Eugene, I may not have had the words for this before now, but I need to tell you that you have so much to offer me, and the entire kingdom of Corona, just by being yourself. Your knowledge of the world from all your adventures, your advice and support and love for me . . . it's everything!"

"You see the best in me," he said, holding me close. "Even when I don't." He kissed my cheek, and before I knew it all my students were applauding. "Rapunzel," he said. "You are my home. I'm sorry."

"Are you with us?" I asked.

"Yes," he said. "I finally did what you've been asking me to this whole trip: listen. And I think I know what the shovels are for."

"What?" I asked.

"I think he wants the kids to harvest the moss," he said. I gasped. Of course! "I saw kids at the bog on my first day, and then, once I truly listened to you and Cass, it all came together. I came as fast as I could."

"We're going to change everything," I said.

Eugene nodded and then took a paintbrush from the pile.

"I can't wait to get my portrait just right," he said. "My hair needs a bit more . . . direction, no?"

"Whatever you say," I answered, and then I laughed, beaming with joy.

34

CASSANDRA

"I see the other side!" I shouted from the front of the boat.

The runaways cheered. We'd conquered the second set of waterfalls. There was still a ways to go, but it appeared we'd reach the village by dawn.

"'I sing a song of the glen, its valleys and hills,'" Stella sang out.

"'We sing a song of the glen, its valleys and hills,'" the rest of the runaways replied.

"'All the riches it holds, in moss and daffodils,'" Stella sang.

And once again the runaways repeated the words back to her.

"'Our hearts are as free as wind through the wheat,'" Stella belted in a voice I'd never heard from her before. "'And no one can trap them, or with darkness defeat.'"

"What is this song?" I asked.

"One of the old songs," Gray said. "We heard our grandparents singing it, but of course it has not been allowed for some time now. Not since the great storm."

It was true that it didn't have even a remotely similar sound to the up-tempo, repetitive songs of Evensing.

They sang the song several more times as the sun rose from behind the mountain.

When we reached the shore, we all jumped out and pulled the log boat onto dry land.

"If we change our minds, we know that it will be waiting for us," Ramona said.

"Actually," Stella said, "I have another idea." She pushed the boat back into the water and gave it a great shove. The runaways cheered and I smiled. They were going to take their village back.

I was about to tell Owl to alert Raps of our arrival, but he was already sailing through the air toward Harmony Glen.

We walked toward the village, and as we did, I could feel a swelling energy. Bits of conversation carried from the other side of the wall. I could hear Rapunzel telling everyone to add as much color as they possibly could. "Let the paint reflect your spirit!" she called.

And then there was silence. Something in the air shifted. The runaways clasped hands. I glanced up at the gate. It was already chained shut.

"What is the meaning of this?" Joaquin's voice burst out.

"We're making a mural, just like you asked us to," Rapunzel replied. Her voice was cheerful, but with an unmistakable note of sternness. "The people's mural needs to represent the people."

"Are we ready?" I whispered. The runaways nodded. "The best kind of attack is a surprise one. We ought to disguise ourselves.

"We'll have to figure out a way to get in," I whispered, gesturing to the locked gate. The runaways nodded.

"We can climb that gigantic tree there," Stella offered.

"If we cover ourselves with dirt and branches, we can reveal ourselves at the perfect moment," I said, thinking quickly.

"Sounds like a plan," Ramona said.

As I gathered leaves and branches, it dawned on me—I was going to be a tree. *Great.* I cringed a little as I realized the play had turned out to be one of my most valuable tools in this coup.

"Unless this mural is whitewashed and returned to order, everyone involved in this will be reduced to a zero-star status," Joaquin's voice boomed over the wall.

"But Joaquin," Rapunzel protested as the runaways and I covered ourselves with mud and leaves, "that's half of your people."

I nodded to the others once more. This was our moment. We stealthily climbed the large tree, helping one another find footholds and handholds.

"Dear, beautiful Princess," Joaquin began. "You have nothing but gold in that pretty heart of yours. However, we do things a little differently here. I tried to explain this you, but I must not have done a very good job."

"'I sing a song of the glen, its valleys and hills,'" Stella sang out as she reached a high branch.

A few voices sang back. "'We sing a song of the glen, its valleys and hills.'"

I peered over the wall at Raps's face, which was bright with wonder.

"What?" Joaquin asked. "What is this? Who is that? Make yourself known!"

"'All the riches it holds, in moss and daffodils,'" the runaways sang out as they balanced in the trees.

The people on the other side of the wall sang back again—and now there were more voices. The song filled the air.

"You heard Joaquin," I whispered to my band of rebels. "It's time to make ourselves known."

Gray was first, jumping from a branch to the top of the wall. I held my breath as he did, but he stuck his landing and then climbed down the wall. As Stella continued to sing the traditional song, I wove my fingers together and offered Ramona my hand. She made her way to the wall, too, and waved triumphantly when she got there. Stella's face was beaming as she sang, and the voices swelled like a wave. Joaquin called for everyone to stop, but no one did.

"It's your turn," I said to Stella. "For Wolf."

Stella nodded and shimmied from her high perch to the wall. The crowd cheered for her and she lowered herself inside the border of Harmony Glen. As I jumped to the wall, and the song continued in a loop, I watched the runaways embracing their loved ones. Joaquin, red-faced and gesturing wildly, was in a huddle with the rest of the village council. Rapunzel hugged me as I hopped down.

"We did it," she said, embracing me.

Eugene was behind her, singing right along with everyone else. And behind him was Joaquin, who had stormed away from the huddle and was now walking straight toward us with a murderous look in his eye.

"Let's not count our chickens before they're—" I began.

"You!" he said, pointing a finger at me. "You started this, didn't you?"

35

EUGENE

"I started nothing!" Cassandra shouted at Joaquin. "I just refused to remain silent."

Joaquin, still red-faced and charged with anger, began to speak, but a woman—who looked exactly like a female version of Wolf—stepped forward.

"And we won't be silenced any longer, either. We didn't run away."

The other people who had climbed the wall with Cassandra joined her. They all linked arms.

I squeezed Rapunzel's hand, and she squeezed mine back. She'd been right all along. I should have known!

I looked at the shining faces around us and

realized that at the same time, there had been something good about this place, too. It was evident in the way that the people cared for those around them, in Lance and Hook Foot's joy, in the natural beauty everywhere. Rapunzel was so amazing about always seeing the best in everyone and everything. I hoped she understood why I'd been so devoted to Harmony Glen.

Cassandra nudged the guy standing next to Wolf's sister. *Speaking of Wolf,* I thought as I scanned the crowd, *where is he?*

I spotted him in the distance. He was so stunned he appeared to be frozen.

"We were taken from Harmony Glen when we deviated from Joaquin's plans or stood out in any way," the man said. "He hired someone to transport us beyond the falls. The village council must have been involved! And now they've locked us all in!"

He pointed at the gates. A collective gasp echoed through the crowd. My pulse quickened. Had I really been so involved in a play about Flynn Rider that I'd missed this? But more importantly, were these people all okay? My heart sank as I thought about their families, who had certainly been missing them.

"Gray!" Abigail said as she stepped forward, away

from Joaquin's huddle. "Do you really think I would have ever been a part of your disappearance?"

"I don't know anymore," Gray said as he wiped tears from his face. "I've been living in the wilderness for so long."

"Never!" Abigail said. "I always thought it was you who wanted to leave, because you didn't love me once I joined the village council. We were betrothed, Gray!"

Rapunzel and I moved an inch closer to each other.

"The drama!" Lance exclaimed under his breath. "The pheasant minder never knew about this, or he would have put the pheasants to work!"

Pascal, caught up in the moment, clasped his heart. Owl looked straight ahead, ever on duty, though even he ruffled his feathers a bit.

Rapunzel and I clasped hands as Gray and Abigail embraced.

"My dear, what happened?" Gray asked as he stroked Abigail's hair.

"Nothing at all," Joaquin said, stepping forward. There was a storm in his normally sunny blue eyes. "This is simply a display of dramatics. Young love! It's like a drug, blinding the senses to truth, reason, and sense."

"No, it's not," I said, speaking with conviction

because I knew exactly what I was talking about. "Real love is a truth potion. The emotions are so pure, anything but the utmost honesty feels like dust on the heart."

"Such poetry," Lance said, shaking his head at the beauty of it all.

"I could write a song!" Hook Foot exclaimed. "Or do an interpretive dance!"

"He's right!" Rapunzel said. "Abigail, what is your truth?"

"What do you know?" I asked.

"I was bullied," Abigail said. She and Gray wove their fingers together. She pointed a finger at Joaquin. "By him. He's going to close our borders forever and sell our most precious resource to a thief."

The crowd gasped.

"It's true," Rapunzel said. "I've seen the plans. He has been distracting you with this festival. He wants to be the only one who's allowed to come and go, all while selling the blue moss to outsiders for money."

The townspeople whispered around us.

"She's a fool! Under the spell of love!" Joaquin blurted out, his face growing redder.

"No, she's not," said Martina. "You bullied me, too. You threatened to banish my family if I revealed that all of the shovels the kids have been making are for harvesting the blue moss."

"But isn't the blue moss what maintains the delicate balance of our ecosystem?" Molly asked.

"Isn't it the very substance that the Author, my great-grandfather, said protected Harmony Glen from greed and ugliness?" Ramona added. "That and our free and open borders, which welcome anyone with a dream!"

"It's too late," Wolf said, at last speaking up. "He made a deal with one of the most notorious thieves in the land. He promised to provide all of the blue moss in our land. Together, they're going to make swords and armor out of it."

"He's even built a secret tunnel for transport," Cassandra added.

"Wolf!" Stella said. "How do you know this?"

"Because he bullied me, too," Wolf said.

There was a pause. And then he added, "After Alfonso blindfolded you, I transported you beyond the falls."

"Oh, Wolf," Abigail said.

"I knew you made that boat," Stella said. "But I didn't think. . . . And yet, yes, how would anyone else know to find me in Grandmother's studio? Wolf, how could you?"

"Stella," Wolf said, "I didn't think I had another choice. I was afraid he would hurt you. At least this way, I could control how you were captured."

"And brought to the middle of the woods?" Stella said, tears streaming down her face.

"Together," Cassandra said. "He made sure you could find one another."

"That's right," Wolf said. "His instructions were to isolate you . . . but instead, I dropped you close enough to come together."

"He tried his best," Gray said. "Clearly Joaquin had not left him with much choice."

Stella still looked hurt, but there was a hint of understanding in her eyes.

"But the stars!" Joaquin said, his voice threaded with desperation. "These people have no stars. Their word is dirt!"

"Even better—our word is moss!" Abigail said.

"Hear, hear!" the people called.

"I think you should tell the story of Ramona, the one that's been omitted from the library," Rapunzel said, leaning into me.

"Yes, please do!" Ramona said.

"With pleasure!" I said. I looked into Rapunzel's sparkling eyes. "And here I thought maybe you were getting tired of Flynn Rider."

"How could I ever grow tired of Flynn Rider?" she asked. I laughed. "But, Eugene," she whispered as she pulled me close. "No imaginary hero could ever compare to you."

She kissed me and the crowd cheered. Then I began to tell the story of *Ramona and the Seven Dragons*.

36
CASSANDRA

When the townspeople had ripped down the chart of stars, Joaquin hadn't protested. If he had put up a fight when Wolf and the others gleefully tore the chart to pieces, we would have gotten him right away. Instead, Joaquin had just stood there, occasionally nodding, as though he were taking the whole scene in, contemplating the situation, and perhaps even coming around to the new state of things. Eugene hopped up on a makeshift stage and dove into the role of Flynn Rider. The townspeople gathered around him to listen.

As Eugene reenacted the story, with Lance playing the role of the dragon king and Hook Foot adding some interpretive dance along the way, Joaquin stood silently in back of the group. Daphne and Molly ran up on the stage to be the baby drag-ons, while Ramona played the character for which she had been named, and Carole whipped out her guitar to provide adventurous music.

Even though *Ramona and the Seven Dragons* was turning out to be my favorite Flynn Rider story so far, I knew I had to keep my eye on Joaquin.

"Look at him, just standing there," I said to Rapunzel, casting a furtive glance at the fallen leader, who appeared to be listening to the story just like any other citizen—as if he hadn't been plotting to crush the spirit of this town.

"I see him," Rapunzel said.

"I should capture him right now," I said. "Knock him out the way he did me. Max and I can take him far away, where I'm sure he'll have to explain to some thugs why he doesn't have their moss, and how he can't get rich by selling what isn't his."

"Cass, it's not our place to decide his fate," Raps said.

"He can't stay here," I said.

"It's their job to determine how to handle this," Raps replied, gesturing to the people.

I frowned, considering this. "You know, I think you're right," I said. If there was one thing I'd learned on this little detour it was that I needed to let other people call the shots sometimes. Still, I gritted my teeth in annoyance. I'd have loved to have locked Joaquin up for good with my own hands.

"But it doesn't mean we can't keep an eye on him," Raps said, and she gestured toward the wall.

I smiled in agreement. As I climbed back up the wall, where I had a view of the scene below, it occurred to me that Raps was getting more accustomed to her role as princess.

Makes my job easier, I thought as I surveyed the glen, though a chill went through me. If she didn't need my guidance, would I still have a role in the kingdom? My eyes drifted to her, and just then, she pointed to Joaquin.

He was walking away at a pace that would suggest he was simply on his way to lunch, though I knew he was trying to get away. "Seize him!" I said as Joaquin tried to make a break for it. He clearly had a warrior's mind.

"Seize him now!" I said again. Gray, Wolf, and Stella leapt into action, tackling Joaquin before he could get too far. The townspeople cheered again.

"This is madness," Joaquin said as Wolf held him back. "With no one to lead you, there will be chaos!"

"I don't think so," Gray said.

"We'll create a new government," Ramona said. "As the Author wrote, 'There's no such thing as flawlessness, and desire for it belies an emptiness I hope you never know.'"

"You don't have the wits to form a government of your own," Joaquin said as he attempted to kick Wolf, who was too quick on his feet for any of Joaquin's blows to land.

"We'll create one in good time," Stella said. "We'll put thought and heart behind our decisions."

"We shall have leaders who change every few years," Martina added.

"And hold fair and free elections," Edmond said.

"We'll write a mission statement," Carole added. "A constitution!"

"Hear, hear!" cried the townspeople.

"And you can't come back here," Molly said, crossing her arms.

"You'll have to stay far away from us!" Daphne said, throwing an arm around her sister.

"I can take him far away," I said. "After I blindfold him and spin him around, he'll have no idea where he's headed. I figure he should know how that feels."

"Let me do the honors," Gray said, whipping out a dark cloth and rolling up his sleeves. "I know just the spot for him."

"And on your return, Gray, we'll have the festival you all deserve!" Rapunzel said.

"But first," Edmond said, commanding the crowd in his loudest voice yet, "let us knock down this gate for good and invite all who want to join our festival to enter Harmony Glen! No one will ever lock us in!"

The cheers were almost deafening!

37
RAPUNZEL

"**H**old on tight," I said to Daphne as she clung to my back. She had decorated my hair with flowers for the smashing of the lock and removal of the gate, and I had promised her a ride! She squealed with delight as she held on to my shoulders and I used my hair to swing us to the top of the wall.

"Woo-hoo!" she shouted as we flew through the air. We high-fived at the highest point of the wall. "I love this view!"

"Me too!" I said, her joy magnifying my own.

Gray, Ramona, and Stella were going to ride Joaquin out of town with the help of Max and

Fidella. We'd hang around the village until they came back, and then be on our own merry way. After all, our journey had deep and serious purpose. We'd had work to do in Harmony Glen—important work—but the fate of Corona was in our hands. It was time to get back to the rocks and discover their meaning. I knew it wasn't going to be an easy road ahead, that there would be bumps and quick decisions. But I was ready.

"Grace, Molly, come on up!" Daphne called, throwing a rope to her sisters. They climbed up to join us and together we applauded the efforts of the people of Harmony Glen.

"Break the lock!" Carole chanted, and soon the rest of the townspeople joined her.

"Are you ready to do the honors?" I asked Daphne, Molly, and Grace as I showed them how to reverse their moss spades and use them like hammers instead. "Come on, girls! Take the first whack at this gate!"

"Yes!" Daphne said, raising the shovel high in the air and knocking the lock. Her sisters joined in and after a few moments of glorious smashing, the lock came off!

"They did it!" I called to the townspeople below. "Storm the gates!"

"Hey, hold your horses, peachy!" called a familiar voice from right outside the border wall.

"Who is that?" Molly asked, peering over the wall from behind my skirts. "She looks like a prune!"

"Is that . . . ?" I squinted to get a better look. "Pearly?"

"The one and only," Pearly replied, dusting off her pantaloons. She spit some sunflower seed shells on the ground and then crushed them with the pointy toe of her boot.

"Hold on!" I called. "Max, Fidella, halt!"

"What's going on, Rapunzel?" Eugene asked. He'd scaled the wall so quickly I hadn't even heard him coming. Even better, Edmond had joined him

"Pearly's down there. I didn't want her to get crushed," I said. I nodded at Edmond, who put two fingers between his lips and issued the loudest whistle I'd ever heard. "Quiet" Edmond was truly quiet no more. The horses stopped in their tracks.

"Hiya, handsome," Pearly said, shading her eyes as she gazed up at Eugene. She spit one last sunflower seed shell in the dirt and flashed a toothy grin. "Tell me, sonny, are you getting a good look at a lady with deep pockets and a taste for the dark side?"

"Um . . . hi?" Eugene said, and shot me a confused look. I shrugged.

"Pearly, have you come for the music and festivities from the old days?" I asked. "If so, you're just in time. We're about to—"

"Girly-girl, I came for my money," Pearly said, whipping out a slingshot and aiming it right at my face. "And by money, I mean moss."

"Hold your fire!" Cass said, drawing back her bow.

"And hold your words, too," I said. "We'll start with diplomacy. Let's be clear. You're the one Joaquin is selling the moss to?" I asked.

"Yes indeedy, sweetie," she said, lunging and taking aim.

"Not so fast," Cass said, aiming an arrow.

"So that's how the village council knew we were coming that first day," Eugene said as we lowered Daphne, Molly, and Grace back down to safety. "She tipped them off!"

"Pearly Perlson gave us away!" I said, shaking my head in disbelief. "She's the big thug behind this whole operation."

"Hey, Chit 'n' Chat! I don't appreciate the holdup. I got a slingshot and I ain't afraid to sling a shot. Send my partner out here with proof of that moss, or Princess Perfect might find herself one eye short of a purty face," Pearly said.

"Pearly, this time it's *you* who decided to bicker

with the wrong biddy," I said, using my hair to swoop down and pick her up, just as Eugene called out "Charge!" to Max and Fidella. The gates opened. I dropped Pearly on Fidella's back.

"What are you trying to tell me, Sassy Sassafras? The deal is dead?" Pearly asked.

"Dead as can be," I said. "Harmony Glen is returning to its natural state of liveliness and love."

"Booooring!" Pearly said. "That's what I have to say about goodness."

"I guess you'll have to find your entertainment elsewhere," I said. "Fidella, she and Joaquin can't be relocated close to one another. We don't need them in cahoots again. Got it?"

Fidella whinnied and nodded.

"Lancey! Lancey! Where are ya?" Pearly called as Ramona tied her to the saddle.

"I'm right here," Lance said, approaching her, his face sagging with disappointment. "Grandma, why'd you tell me you were on the straight and narrow if you were still down and dirty?"

"I thought I was on the good path, sonny boy. But sometimes badness is in the bones," Pearly remarked, flexing her biceps. "What do you say? Join me. We could make a pretty penny together, the two of us. I still have a few tricks up my poet's blouse sleeve."

"Sorry, Granny," Lance said. "I have real friends now, and that's better than any treasure I've ever found. I can't give them up, not for all the gold in the world."

"Good for you," Pearly said, and then grimaced. "I guess."

"If I were going to break bad for anyone, it'd be you, Pearly. But those days are over for me," Lance said.

Pearly nodded, dejected but understanding. She waved Lance off.

"Hey, handsome," Pearly called to Eugene. Eugene turned to her, surprised. Pearly winked and blew him a kiss. "I just needed one last glance at that magnificent mug for the road."

"I'm not sure about how I feel about all of this," Eugene said to me. I held his hand.

"Take it as a compliment," I said.

"Hi-dee-ho!" Pearly called, whooping as Max and Fidella rode off.

"No doubt they'll be taken very far away," Cassandra said as the townspeople stepped out from behind the wall and watched them take off in the direction of the waterfall.

We all watched them go. Max and Fidella seemed to be galloping faster than ever before with Joaquin and Pearly on their backs. Maybe they'd missed the open road, too. Maybe perfect carrots and apples weren't what they really wanted, deep in their hearts. We'd all be out on the open road again soon enough. We had a mission, and it was where we belonged.

"Old Pearly," Lance mused, shaking his head. "And here I thought she'd reformed."

"Some actors just can't give up their roles," Hook Foot added.

"Hey, speaking of actors," Eugene said, "I believe we have a performance to put on!"

"Oh, yes!" Alfonso said. "And this time, I think you should use all the quotes you know. The *real* ones."

"Carole," I called, "play us a tune as we walk to the theater!"

"I can do that," Carole said, strapping on her guitar and plucking a tune. "And this time I think I'll improvise."

She played a happy song, and the townspeople followed her toward the village.

I noticed Cass lagging behind. She appeared to be gathering sticks. "Hey, Cass, are you coming?"

"Yeah," she said, holding up branches. "Just making sure I have the best costume possible."

I laughed until I cried.